The Lie in Our Hearts

The Lie in Our Hearts

EVELYN LANDY

SKY
PUBLISHING HOUSE
NEW YORK

Published by
Sky Publishing House LLC
New York, NY
www.skypublishinghouse.com

Publisher's Cataloging-in-Publication Data
Landy, Evelyn.

The lie in our hearts / Evelyn Landy. – New York, NY :
Sky Pub. House LLC, 2019.

p. ; cm.

ISBN13: 978-0-9600933-0-4

1. Teenage girls--Fiction. 2. Female friendship--Fiction.
3. Best friends--Fiction. I. Title.

PS3612.A63 L54 2019
813.6--dc23

Project coordination by Jenkins Group, Inc.
www.BookPublishing.com

Interior design by Brooke Camfield

Printed in the United States of America
23 22 21 20 19 • 5 4 3 2 1

Prologue

The only time it's ever busy in East Shore is the summer, when people come for the beach. This town is supposed to be a cute little vacation spot, but when winter comes around, it feels empty and small. I've been to the city a bunch of times to visit my cousins, and even though they are only one hour away, it feels like they live in a completely different, exciting place.

I've always wanted to get out of this small town. That may be why the movie theater was one of my favorite places. That was where I really decided I wanted to become a storyteller. During junior year, I'd go to the theater and stay for hours, to the point where everyone there knew my name. Then I found a new love of words, which brought me to the library. I read books and held onto words in a way I never had before. Maybe I was reluctant to go to the library before because they didn't have the best kids' section. Or maybe I didn't know how to appreciate books yet. But I got older and grew to love stories and reading, which led me to writing.

In my senior year, I told my friends that I wanted to apply to colleges and become a writer. It was a big surprise, because they knew that when I'd first started writing, I hated it. I thought I had nothing to say. It took me awhile to realize it, but East Shore actually gave me complex characters with compelling stories. I couldn't even begin to imagine what my life would be like if I made it out of this town and to a big city with all of those people and all of their stories.

And, so, I've decided that I'll start by telling my own story, of the year that I had gone to a writing club for the first time and almost threw every document I wrote into the trash. It was the year that I almost lost myself and the sight of my dreams.

I know that to everyone else, my life as a sixteen-year-old looked like silly high school girl drama. But why does high school girl drama always seem silly to anyone looking in from the outside? After everything that happened with my friends and me, we decided to find the things that we actually liked to do. If all the drama taught me anything, it was that I had a voice, and there was no reason not to share it.

One

One Wednesday afternoon in February, my school decided to have a Q&A with the newly elected mayor. It didn't make much sense to me because he had already won the job. We gathered for the assembly in the auditorium, and when I realized that it was going to be about politics, I took out my phone to finish the cheesy Netflix rom-com I'd started the night before when I was *supposed* to be doing my chemistry homework. That was the life of any teenage hopeless romantic, and I was one by definition.

I was the quiet girl who watched too many rom-coms and fell for the guy on-screen, only to have her heart broken every time the credits rolled. I was the girl who at fifteen had realized she was never going to have one of those perfect movie love stories and she just had to live with it.

"Would you mind turning your phone off? It's very disrespectful," a teacher said.

I froze. I didn't even bother to see which teacher had busted me as I stuffed my phone into my backpack. I could feel my cheeks getting bright red, but it was okay because it was too dark in the auditorium for anyone else to see my face. I had just made it too easy for myself to get caught.

It didn't help that after I put my phone away and gave my attention to the front, I realized that Jack Walker was sitting right in front of me, whispering some undeniably stupid joke to his friends. I'd finally suppressed my crush for him after all of these years. It took all of middle school, a year and a half of high school, and all of his ex-girlfriends for me to realize that it would never happen. It didn't bother me anymore, but a part of me wished it did.

I turned my attention away from Jack, something I'd had much practice with, and thought about the creative writing club, which I was planning on joining later that day in an attempt to buff up my extracurriculars, even though a large part of me figured I wouldn't have the courage to walk through the door.

When I walked into the classroom, the first face I saw was Jack's. I froze. I'd had classes with him over the years, but I tried to block him out and ignore his stupid jokes. We locked eyes for only a second, but that was all it took for my crush on him to come rushing back. I didn't want to maintain eye contact with him, mainly because his eyes were the softest shade of blue I'd ever seen and I didn't know what I'd do if he looked at me one more time. Things were so much easier when I was staring at his back in the auditorium. The truth was undeniable, though. I still had a massive crush on him, and I couldn't push it away anymore—except, knowing me, I probably would.

Like I said, I was the quiet girl, and I had never said more than a couple of words to him. I was going to sit a few seats over, but the chairs were turned in a circle rather than a grid, which gave me a kind of courage that took us both by surprise. "Can I sit here?" I asked pointing to the seat next to him.

He nodded, but he was focused on a notebook that was stuffed with scraps of paper from everywhere. I saw some napkins from restaurants around town, but that wasn't even what caught my eye about his notebook. It looked like it had been through hurricanes, coffee spills, and tornadoes, but by some miracle, it was still in one piece—kind of.

That's when I remembered having seen Jack sign up for this writing group at the club fair last September. I was signing up for the school paper that I didn't actually plan on participating in. The next booth over was for the creative writing club, and it seemed as though Jack was mesmerized by what the girl in charge was telling him. Then his wannabe jock friends came by and made fun of him. He started laughing too, and then they all walked away. Fifteen minutes later, I was signing up for another club I didn't plan on participating in (fashion club, maybe) when I saw Jack come back to sign up for the creative writing club. I remembered smiling to myself, because maybe he wasn't the conceited jerk who only cared about what his friends thought. To my surprise, I hadn't thought about that in over a year.

"So do you come here a lot?" Once I asked the question, I realized it may have sounded desperate.

"I forgot my AirPods," Jack said, digging into his backpack.

I sat back in my seat, believing that my whole fantasy about him wouldn't actually happen. But on the bright side, he probably hadn't heard my desperate pickup line.

Thankfully, there wasn't much downtime to try to fill the silence with a forced conversation between us. The girl, who was the leader of the club, introduced herself as Cynthia, a senior.

She welcomed us to the group, and we did the thing where everyone in the circle took turns saying their names and their grades. I was last. "Bella Carter," I said. "Sophomore."

"Perfect," Cynthia said, too bubbly. She said there weren't really any rules or restrictions to our writing and we should just write whatever came to our minds. She got up and scribbled the day's prompt in big, loopy letters: "The Universe."

I opened my computer to a new document and stared at the blank screen. I looked over at Jack, but he was too busy scribbling furiously in his notebook. The universe, I thought, that was kind of broad. I looked back at Jack to see him scribbling furiously—still. I wondered how he had so much to say when I had so little. And, then, I had a strange surge of inspiration, and I started writing a weird piece about how I felt trapped in my universe and couldn't escape.

When our time was up, I grew embarrassed when I quickly skimmed my piece over. When Cynthia asked who would like to share, I kept staring at my computer and avoided eye contact. That was when Jack nudged me and said, "Why don't you share, Bella?" It was weird to hear my name on his lips. I didn't think he'd ever said it. It was funny, though, because there weren't that many kids in my grade and everybody knew everybody, so he would have had to have said it at some point.

"Why don't you go?" I asked.

"Okay," Jack said, folding his notebook back with a confidence like he'd done it many times before. He described being stuck in a universe, so that was something we had in common. He spoke with an eloquence that I thought I'd never achieve, but that was fine because this was his thing. While I was listening, I couldn't help but notice something thumping against my desk, but it was quiet enough for no one else to hear, except for Jack. I managed to sneak a glance under the desk, and, sure enough, his leg was bouncing up and down nervously—so maybe he did have flaws after all. The rest of the club meeting was a blur of positive feedback, and Jack kept a smug look on his face, as though he was expecting exactly that. Then Cynthia thanked everyone for coming, but something was bothering me.

I couldn't remember most of what he had said except for his main point, that he felt trapped. I just didn't understand how. The other club members left pretty quickly, leaving the two of us alone to pack up our things and part our separate ways. That's what I thought would happen too, except it didn't. Jack started moving the desks back, and the trapped thing was still bothering me. After that night, I probably wouldn't be speaking to Jack again, because while the club was nice and all, I didn't think creative writing was my thing. I just decided to take a chance and ask him about it.

"Were you not listening to what I just said?" he asked me, as if he wasn't really in the mood to repeat his entire poem—I think it was a poem. I took another risk, which seemed to be a theme that day.

"I mean, you use a lot of figurative language and metaphors and stuff, but what are you actually trying to say?" I asked.

"Wow."

"Thanks for the *great* answer," I said. He laughed.

"Sorry, it's just that when you put 'figurative language and metaphors and stuff' on paper, people never really question it. They just tell me I'm a good writer."

"Stop," I said, hitting him playfully, except I didn't end up hitting him playfully. It was kind of an awkward hit, and he laughed again. I was surprised when it didn't seem like he was laughing at me, more at the situation, so I laughed with him.

"Sorry," I said after I took a deep breath.

"You're funny, Bella," he said.

"No one ever tells me that," I said. It was true, except for my five-year-old brother, who found my awkwardness hilarious.

"Well, maybe people just don't know you well enough," he said.

"Yeah," I nodded in agreement.

"So . . . " he said, him being the one in an uncomfortable situation for once. He looked like he was building up courage, a foreign look for him. "Do you want to grab some pizza so I can tell you more about 'figurative language and metaphors and stuff'?"

"Stop making fun of me," I told him, laughing.

Then I replayed what he had just asked me. Did he ask me out? I had never been asked out. I'd never been kissed, I'd never held a conversation with a boy longer than this, and here he was asking me out . . . I think. I didn't know enough to tell, so I just went along with it and said, "Sure."

"Okay, I just need to get my jacket from my locker, and then I'll meet you outside," he said.

"Okay, bye, Jack." At first, it felt weird to say his name out loud, because I had said it so often to myself for years, but then he smiled at me. I felt like I would be saying his name a thousand times more, as if it were my favorite word.

I replayed what had just happened in my head. I was still in the same exact place from when he asked me out, or whatever that was. If I had known it would be so easy, I would've talked to him years ago. Maybe my life would've been different and I'd be a different person. Someone who was more confident, had guy friends, went to parties, things like that. I couldn't deny that there was something special about it happening on that specific night, like it had been fate or destiny. It wasn't forced or planned. As much as I wished it had happened sooner, I wouldn't have wanted it any other way. I'd always wanted a romantic story, and there it was, but I was getting ahead of myself. The boy asked me to pizza, most likely as friends, because he'd had girlfriends so much prettier and much more popular than me. Every time I'd seen him walking around school last year with his arm around a girl, I couldn't help but feel a pang of jealousy.

I pushed the thought out of my head as I grabbed my jacket from the back of my chair and walked slowly out of the room. I was going to get pizza with Jack Walker. I was still stunned. But then I couldn't help but think, what if it was all some practical joke, like he'd ditch me and pretend we never talked to each other?

To my relief, he was standing at the end of the hallway, right by the building's doors. He kept his hands in his jacket pockets and was staring off into space, maybe still thinking about how he felt trapped. It felt nice to see Jack with a genuine look on his face, and I didn't want to forget it. Jack noticed me staring and gave me a little wave. We opened the door, and the cold February air blew in our faces, but I didn't mind it because winter had always been my favorite season. It wasn't warm one day and cold another like with spring and fall. Summer was too warm. It was supposed to be a time for sunshine and fun—but it wasn't always that way. With winter, I knew exactly what it was, cold and brutal, but at least you knew it was coming.

"So you wanna go to Tony's?" Jack asked. It was too dark to tell, but I think he was blushing—either that or the cold air was making his cheeks red. Tony's was the only pizza place in town and just happened to be a block away, so asking me if I wanted to go there was kind of a stupid question. I think he'd gotten a little nervous around me, which I thought was cute.

"Yeah, Tony's sounds good," I said, as if there were three other pizza places in town.

"Hey, are you cold? You could take my jacket," he said as his teeth chattered. I was starting to see the kinder, softer side of Jack that I hadn't been sure even existed. Under all of his idiocy and arrogance, he was sweet. Boyfriend sweet, but I couldn't think of him like that. It probably wasn't a date, which I told myself repeatedly.

"It's fine; you can keep it. It looks like you need it more than I do."

He sighed with relief and said, "Okay, good." Then we set off to Tony's.

"So you have a brother, right?" That was Jack trying to make small talk, which was better than me trying to make small talk.

"Yeah, Henry." I was kind of surprised he remembered that, but then again, we lived in a small town, so how surprised could I really be?

"Hey, was he—" I knew where this was going; it had pretty much defined my brother for the past three years, not that it wasn't funny "—the kid who drew all over his face with red marker at the middle school Halloween party and said he was Elmo?"

"He was two!" I said, defending my brother, but I couldn't hide the happiness in my voice.

"So it was him. That little dude cracked me up. I swear that whole year whenever I needed a good laugh, I'd think about him."

"Wasn't that the year that—" I stopped myself because that wasn't something I was used to talking about.

"The year my parents got divorced? Yeah," Jack said as if it was no big deal, but I could tell it was.

And then we reached Tony's. He held the door for me, and I was surprised by this whole new Jack. We walked over to the counter, but before we ordered, Jack looked at me.

"I'm starting to think this was a mistake," he told me.

I couldn't believe it. Maybe it was because I brought up the divorce thing. Just when I was starting to think that he was a whole other person.

"What do you mean?" I asked, unable to hide the hurt in my eyes.

He looked at me for a second, and his whole expression changed into something more apologetic. "Oh, you think I'm talking about—no, no, I meant going for pizza. I shoulda said sushi or something because I have this really weird thing, and all of my friends make fun of me for it, but I like putting potato chips on my pizza."

I couldn't hold back my smile. "Are you serious? It's so good!" I used to put chips on my pizza all of the time when I was little when I'd spend the summers with my cousins in New York City."

"You're joking. You've actually had pizza with chips?" he asked, excited.

"Yeah, do you ever do it with ice cream?"

"Ice cream, pizza, and potato chips, hmm . . . never thought about it," he said.

"No, I meant just ice cream and—" I paused. Jack was about to burst into laughter. He had a funny, scrunched up expression on his face, and I couldn't help but laugh. Then he started laughing too.

"Are you two going to order or what?" Tony came out of the bustling kitchen to help us out at the counter. And, yes, the guy who owned Tony's was actually named Tony. One of the many pleasures of a small town, I guess.

Jack turned around to face him. "Yeah, sorry."

"Oh, great, it's Jack Attack," Tony said. Then he looked at me and asked, "New girlfriend?"

9

Before I could react, Jack told Tony, "It isn't like that; she's just a friend." I didn't know whether to be happy or upset. There was still a part of me that didn't want Jack to think of me as just a friend, but that was going to be a long shot. "Okay, so we're gonna get two slices and two bags of chips?" he asked me, and then I realized he was waiting for my approval, so I nodded.

"Oh, and a water," I said.

"Okay, so two waters," he told Tony and then turned to me, as I started to reach for my wallet. "It's on me. Why don't you go grab us a table?" I turned around to see that the place was unusually quiet for a Wednesday evening at 5:30, but I went to sit at a booth anyway.

Once Tony got the pizzas, the chips, and the water bottles, he clicked some buttons on his ancient cash register. Jack paid and brought the tray with all of our food to the table.

We ate in silence, but then our eyes locked once we got to the crust of our slices and we couldn't contain our laughter anymore. I loved making Jack laugh. It didn't seem like an achievement anymore, rather something I enjoyed doing and wanted to do for a long time. But, first, I had to ask him a question.

I tried asking casually. "So, um, the first girl you brought here. Who was that?"

"What girl?" he asked. So much for being casual.

"The girl," I said, really hoping he was going to answer.

"What girl?"

Great, was he really going to ask me again? He must've read my face as he answered, "oh yeah, you mean the thing Tony said," he said. He cleared his throat. "That would be, um . . . Leanne."

Leanne was my ex-best friend. We were the type of best friends where people envied our relationship because we were so close, until everything changed when we got to high school. To make a long story short: we fought, Leanne got new and better friends, and she started dating Jack. I hadn't talked to her since and didn't plan on talking to her anytime soon, and it seemed like Jack didn't either.

"What were we talking about again?" I asked after a pause.

"Leanne."

"Oh, right."

"Hey, do you mind if we switch the topic?" That's when I saw it in his eyes—hurt. I knew that Leanne cheated on him, but I didn't think that he was still hung up about it.

"Yeah, I believe you were going to tell me about 'figurative language and metaphors and stuff,'" I said.

"So you want to know what my poem really meant?"

So it was a poem. "Yeah."

"Okay, so my parents got divorced when I was in seventh grade. When my dad moved out, he wanted me to move in with him so I could 'have a man in the house.' My mom said she would be okay on her own if I lived with my dad, so that's what I did. It wasn't working out, though, because my dad always forgot to pick me up for school, he went to bars and got drunk, and then he'd bring home a different girl every night who looked closer to my age than his. You get what I'm saying, right?"

I was surprised. Yes, I knew his parents got divorced and Leanne cheated on him, but despite this, I always thought he had a perfect life. Looking back, I didn't know how I formulated that opinion, but that didn't matter. I gave him a slight nod, so he continued.

"I ended up staying with my mom, permanently. She met this guy, Dave, and they started dating. A few weeks after they started dating, my dad called and said he wanted to hang out and take me out to a basketball game. He'd started to fix his life and got a new job that just happened to involve season tickets to box seats. So, of course, I said yes, and it became a weekly thing.

11

I was starting to consider staying at my dad's every other week-end or something like that.

"Then my mom got engaged to Dave. My dad started asking me questions about Dave and how my mom was doing, and he started telling me to tell my mom that he missed her. Instead of watching the games, all he'd do was talk about my mom, so I eventually realized he was using me and told him to back off. I didn't see him for a while, and I was busy helping my mom with the wedding, and because I wasn't spending so much time with my dad anymore, I started talking to Dave. He was a really decent guy, the exact opposite of my dad. He was kind of a nerd, but I think that's what my mom needed. The wedding was a few months ago at my house, in September. So, anyway, it's the reception, and everyone's having a good time. That is, until my dad comes in drunk off his ass and starts asking my mom to give him another chance. I needed to get away from all of the drama, so I started to look for my friends, who I realized I hadn't seen in a while. And I found them, in my room. Mark and Leanne were making out on my bed. So, anyway, what I was trying to say was that I'll always be trapped in this universe where people see me as the son of the crazy drunk dad and the kid whose girlfriend cheated on him with his best friend. Hey, do you mind saying something now?" He asked this as if the last thing he wanted to do was sit in silence.

"I'm sorry," I said. What else was I supposed to say?

"No, Bella, I don't want to be that guy. Just tell me about you. What's your story?"

"It's going to sound petty compared to yours."

"No, it won't. Just . . . say anything that's been on your mind. It'll feel really good once you tell *someone*." He smiled at me, like I was special, but I didn't have some special story. All I had was petty girl drama.

"You don't mind if I talk about Leanne a little?"

"Nah, I talked about her a little too."

I started to tell Jack about my friendship with Leanne and how it began to change.

"Bella, I know about Leanne. In fact, I think everyone in the entire school knows about your friendship with Leanne. Tell me something I don't know, something deep and personal. Tell me something you've never told anyone before."

"But you didn't tell me something you've never told anyone before."

"Yeah, I, uh, did—remember the thing about my dad? I never told anyone what happened when I was living with him or what happened at the basketball games. As far as anyone knows, I moved back in with my mom because it was closer to school and my friends, and I had fun at the games, but I wasn't spending enough time on my homework, so I had to stop."

"Did you tell your mom the truth?"

"I love her, but I didn't want her to hate my dad because of those things, so, no, I never told her."

I felt special. I wasn't expecting that we'd be sharing secrets. Jack was this popular boy whom everyone liked, and there he was, letting all of his defenses down, telling me everything. Maybe it was because we were basically still strangers, even though we sort of knew each other for a long time. Maybe telling a stranger your secrets is like starting fresh, because you're telling things to someone who doesn't know enough to judge you.

I wanted to tell him something I'd never told anyone. "Okay, do you want to hear about my parents?"

"Oh yeah, your dad was the one who scored the winning basket in the championship game of '99 against Leeman High, right?"

"Um . . . I think so. Anyway, my dad kind of reminds me of you. You know, popular, cool, and good-looking—"

"You think I'm 'you know, popular, cool, and good-looking'?" He laughed.

"Jack, shut up! Do you really have to quote me on everything I say?"

"Yes," he said, as a big, mischievous grin spread across his face.

"Just let me finish my story. So my dad's—"

"'You know, popular, cool, and good-looking,'" Jack let out a chuckle. "I said I'd quote you."

"Whatever. My mom was like Leanne, I guess, without the whole cheating thing. I'm like the exact opposite of them, and sometimes I feel like I don't fit in, like I'm the black sheep of the family. Henry's my mom's 'little man,' and my dad always takes him to sports games. I have nothing in common with my parents. It's hard enough to not fit in with your family, but I don't really fit in at school, either. But you're Jack, so you probably wouldn't understand that last part anyway."

"I do. Stop doubting me, Bella," he said. Then, shifting his tone, he said, "If you look past my, you know, popularity, coolness, and good-lookingness—"

"'Good-lookingness' isn't a word!" I laughed.

"Yeah, it is. Look it up in a dictionary."

"Sure," I said sarcastically, but what he didn't know was that I made a mental note to check on that later.

I'd already started telling him my story, so I continued. After my falling out with Leanne, my mom pressured me all year to patch things up. I think the real reason was that my mom wanted me to be more like Leanne, whether it came to her looks or her new friends. It was more than that, though. Leanne was the daughter my mom never had. My mom had grown up with four brothers, and she'd always wanted a daughter to talk about girl stuff with, but I was just not that girl. When Leanne would come over, they would mindlessly talk in the kitchen about the smallest things, things I had no interest in, no matter how much I wished I did. Then I told Jack the scariest part, the part I'd never been able to say aloud—not even to myself—about how sometimes I felt unwanted.

"You know what, Bella? They're wrong, and so are you."

That caught me by surprise. "What am *I* wrong about?"

"In twenty years from now, if I have a daughter, I'd make sure that she'd *never* feel that way." He stood up. "I think I'm gonna go. I'll see you around, okay?"

I'd been "seeing Jack around" for over five years, and I didn't think I could keep doing it anymore. "Jack, wait!"

He turned around with a serious look on his face. Then he broke into laughter. "Gotcha!"

"Jack, you're not funny," I said. In that moment, I had felt really hurt.

"Bella, admit it: I'm hilarious."

"So you're not going?"

"No, I don't have any plans. It's not like my dad's picking me up and taking me to a basketball game."

I must have been giving him a blank stare, because he said, "It was a joke. This is the part where you're supposed to laugh."

We sat back down, and I checked my watch to see that it was 7:00. That meant it was time for Tony's "mood lighting," which meant Tony would go around the restaurant and place cheap candles from Wicker, the candle store across the street, on every table. And that was it, no other lights. We laughed about Tony's mood lighting, and then our conversation started up again.

15

"Hey, Jack Attack, I'm closing. How 'bout you and your girl-friend get outta here?"

"She's not my, um . . . girlfriend," he said a lot less defensively than he had the first time. I couldn't help but feel hopeful, because maybe Jack wanted to be something more than friends, and that thought could probably hold me over for the rest of high school.

I think Tony felt it too, oddly, because he added in, "Yet."

I don't think Jack noticed that he wasn't smiling at him, rather at me. I shot Tony a look, and I think he got the message, because he started to busy himself by sweeping the floors. I got my jacket, and so did Jack, and then we said bye to Tony and left.

"Hey, you live on Elmwood, right?" Jack asked.

"Yeah."

"I could walk you home; it's on my way." He didn't have to tell me that because I already knew that, and he already knew that I knew that.

"Only if you want to," I told him, wondering how our conversation got so awkward.

"I do," he said. "But only if you want me to."

I smiled at the thought of Jack walking me home. "I do."

We walked to my house, quietly, kind of just appreciating nature. At least that's what I was doing. My house wasn't far from Tony's, so when we reached it, I was kind of disappointed and wished that my house had been a couple of miles away rather than a couple of blocks.

"Okay, then, I'll see you around." Jack waved.

It was more than your average "see you around," I could tell. "Yeah, see you around," I said in return.

I walked up my stairs, kind of mindlessly, my mind still occupied with thoughts of Jack. When I went to open my front door, out of the corner of my eye I saw him standing there . . . still. I turned around, and there was Jack, hands in his jacket pockets.

"What are you still doing here?"

"I'm making sure you get inside okay."

I smiled to myself for what must've been the fifth time that night, but I realized I still had one more thing to say to him. "You're right."

"You'll have to be more specific," he said, joking.

That made me laugh. "You'll be a good dad in twenty years."

He grinned but didn't say anything, and for a few seconds neither did I. I wanted to end on a high note, so I said, "Good night, Jack."

I didn't think I was ever going to get tired of saying his name, and when he said, "Good night, Bella," I could tell he wasn't going to get tired of saying mine.

alking to school the next day, I couldn't help but think that my pizza not-date with Jack the night before was a dream. There was no other possible explanation. I had to find some kind of proof, so I unlocked my phone. I didn't have Jack's number, and he didn't have mine. We hadn't taken any pictures of our pizza or poems or anything else to remember the night by. Then it hit me. I opened my web browser, and there it was: the definition of "good-lookingness" on the *Merriam-Webster Dictionary* website. That meant it was all real, from the creative writing club to Tony's, to the walk home, and to saying good night. It was all real.

When I reached school, I reminded myself that it was Thursday. I had no classes with Jack on Thursdays, except for math, which was last period, and that was fine with me. I didn't think I'd be ready to see him any earlier, and it would take me all day to prepare myself to see him. I was never good at talking to people, so if I did run into him, I'd have no idea what I'd say, or I'd be awkward and ruin the easy flow of conversation we'd had the night before.

I also remembered that I hadn't done any of my homework. I'd always been a good student—I mostly got As with a couple of B plusses and A minuses. For the most part, I got the A minuses and B plusses because I didn't participate in class enough. Otherwise, I studied hard. I needed As to get out of this town and go to a good college that was far away from here, where I could get a fresh start. I had no idea what I wanted to do with my life, but one thing was for sure: I wasn't going to be in my hometown forever.

At school, I walked over to Makenzie's locker, which was our "spot." In my friend group, there was Makenzie, the smart one; Jade, the artsy one; and Nicole, the outgoing, boy-crazy one. Leanne had been a part of our group too, until she started dating Jack and "upgraded" her friends.

Everyone else was already there, trying to calm Makenzie down about the ninety-four that she had gotten on her chemistry midterm. Makenzie was crying about how she wasn't ranked first in the class anymore.

"Where were you last night?" Makenzie asked me. "I called you like five times, and you didn't answer."

I was about to come up with some excuse, when out of the corner of my eye, I saw Leanne approaching. Leanne, Jade, and I had history together with Ms. Anderson, whose classroom door was just a few feet away from Makenzie's locker. A lot of people thought that I stopped talking to Leanne because I hated her, but I was just afraid to talk to her. Even after our falling-out, I never hated Leanne. That would be impossible. Leanne was like a sister to me, and it's hard to truly hate your sister. It just seemed like Leanne had changed so much from middle school to high school.

At the beginning of our sophomore year, I had finally worked up the courage to talk to Leanne, but then again, almost overnight, she was transformed into a completely different person.

After Jack's mom's wedding, people started calling her "the sophomore slut." I realized I didn't even recognize her anymore.

That morning, Leanne was wearing tight, dark clothes, along with heavy makeup, her usual uniform. She was good at pretending she didn't hear what people said and walked as though she didn't have a care in the world, while anyone else would have had to put some effort behind it. This bothered me for some reason, and I thought about how I'd hung out with Jack the night before, which made me feel unusually emboldened. I knew what I was about to say would sound petty and desperate, but it didn't seem fair that Leanne could walk around like she owned the place. "Hey, Leanne," I called out. "Jack says he doesn't forgive you yet."

All the chatter and noise around us stopped, and for the first time, I liked the attention.

Leanne stopped walking, but she didn't turn to face us. She held her books to her chest, like she didn't have time to deal with whatever it was I was saying. "You don't want to do this, Bella. Do you really think you're special or something because Jack *finally* noticed you?" she asked. That meant everyone knew, and I became even more bold, despite her "warning." I didn't trust what she said anymore.

"Yeah, we went to Tony's," I said. "He told me *everything*."

"You were too busy having pizza with Jack to help me?" Makenzie asked.

"Jack? As in Jack Walker?" Nicole asked. "Oh my god, he's so hot. Wait, Jack talked to *you*?" She was shocked in an insulting way, but I let it slide.

I thought about what Jack had told me, about how Leanne had no idea about what was going on with him and his dad and how she had hurt him so much. That wasn't the Leanne I knew, the Leanne who wouldn't hurt anyone. She needed to know how it felt.

I caught up with Leanne and shoved her.

"What the hell?" she said, as I caught her off guard.

"How could you?"

"How could I what?"

Despite the fact that she was being completely genuine and didn't know what I was talking about, I still felt disgusted and angry. I couldn't help myself and . . . BAM!

Leanne let out a screech as her left cheek flushed bright red. Everyone turned to see the scene that I had just caused. I realized what I had just done. I had hit Leanne on the cheek, hard. I'd never gotten in trouble, and I'd never been sent to the principal's office. I didn't understand how I lost control, because I *never* lost control.

After I hit Leanne, everything went by in a blur. Ms. Anderson, the teacher who had adored me right up until that moment, was the only teacher at the scene. She separated us and escorted me to the office. When I was being hauled off to the office, I knew that getting caught couldn't have gone any other way. Leanne was never a tattletale, and, in that way, she hadn't changed.

The principal was angry that I had violated the "no tolerance for violence" policy, but then he only gave me a week's worth of detentions rather than the normal suspension he would have given to other kids. I should have been relieved, but in that moment, I didn't want to be the goody two-shoes everyone thought I was. I wished I could be more unpredictable, so that people wouldn't assume that when I did something bad, it was a one-time thing. I knew myself, though. I wouldn't try to do anything to tarnish my image, so I accepted my punishment and went to class.

The day zoomed by, and before I knew it, it was 2:35, which meant I had to be in math class. I had managed to not run into Jack all day, and I considered that an accomplishment. My plan was to be the last one to class without being late, because I didn't like to be late . . . ever. So I went into the classroom just as the bell rang and saw the empty seat a few rows behind mine that belonged to Jack. Jack always came late to class, and that was excluding the times he ditched and didn't bother showing up at all.

That day, though, Jack showed up a lot earlier than usual. I wanted to think that it was because of me, and when he shot me a smile, I couldn't help but believe that theory. In one smooth motion, he took off his backpack. If I had tried that, I would've failed and looked really awkward. Jack's seat was in the back row, of course, because where else would a kid like Jack Walker sit?

I couldn't focus on anything except Jack. I knew that was going to happen, but I couldn't do anything to stop it. I tried to focus on angles, triangles, theorems, and whatever useless information the teacher was going on and on about, but it was impossible. I couldn't help but wonder, was this how Leanne felt when she liked Jack? Somehow, with Jack, everything came back to Leanne.

Out of the corner of my eye, I could see Luke, Jack's annoying friend, lean over with his gray hoodie pulled over his face and whisper to Jack.

"Dude, what's up with you and Bella?" Luke asked, loud enough for me to hear.

"Nothing," Jack whispered.

"Please don't tell me it's like Leanne all over again."

"It's not like that," Jack said. "I took her to Tony's."

"You took *Leanne* to Tony's." Somehow that made me feel better, more hopeful.

"That doesn't mean anything; just relax. She's different," Jack said, stomping out any ounce of hope I had left.

"Hey, Jack, I didn't see it until now, but Bella's kind of hot — not Leanne hot, but in some nerdy kind of way. Besides, did you see how she hit Leanne today? So hot."

"Bella hit Leanne?" I was surprised he didn't hear or see it happen. Maybe he'd been trying to avoid me all day too.

"So you wouldn't mind if I ask her out, right?"

I shuddered at the thought because Luke was notorious for being a womanizer at my school. I wouldn't be caught dead going out with him. Besides, Luke had never gone out with girls who were hot in a "nerdy kind of way," and the only reason he wanted to start was because Jack spoke to me. Then I brightened with how that meant Jack *was* interested in me.

"Hey, dude, can you just shut up about Bella? She'd never go out with you anyway because you're not her type. So just shut up, because maybe I want to learn whatever this dumbo's saying."

That last part Jack said loud enough for the whole class to hear and, more importantly, loud enough for the "dumbo" himself to hear.

"Mr. Walker, what did you just call me?" the teacher asked, turning around from the triangles he'd just drawn on the board.

"Hey, if you heard the rest of the conversation, you'd actually be on my side, uh, sir," Jack said. "You see, I was telling Luke that we should listen to what you have to say—right, man?"

"Hey, don't drag me into this," Luke said, keeping his eyes down on his notebook.

"Mr. Walker, detention."

"Detention?" Jack and I asked at the same time. Jack looked at me, confused. I tried to keep my mouth shut, but I couldn't. Jack couldn't go to detention. It was the day I was trying to get him out of my mind, and yet he kept coming back. Was I supposed to take this as a sign?

"Do you want detention?" the teacher asked, looking at me. I could never remember my math teacher's last name because it was some long, hard-to-pronounce Russian last name, so I stopped trying.

My first response was to say no, but then I realized I already had detention. When you're the quiet kid in class, you learn a few things about how to survive being asked questions you don't know the answer to. For example, pretending to figure out the answer until the teacher gets tired of you and moves onto the next victim.

Unfortunately, the math teacher wasn't satisfied with that and said, "I'm waiting," as if he had all the time in the world.

I looked down at the floor and said quietly, "I already have detention." The teacher mumbled something under his breath in Russian and continued, as if he was satisfied with my answer, while I was kind of ashamed of it.

Throughout the rest of class, I kept being distracted by thoughts of Jack. I wasn't going to be one of the many girls, like Leanne, who changed for some stupid guy, like Jack. Yet there was a small voice in the back of my head that whispered, "Jack isn't some stupid guy." The voice was quiet, and soon I would let that voice get louder and louder and tell me what to do—but that's for later. Once the bell rang, the whole class rushed out of the room. I tried to leave right away and avoid Jack, but he grabbed my arm and looked straight into my eyes with his pale blue ones, and I couldn't leave.

"Bella, you didn't have to hit Leanne for me."

I wanted to say something like, "I didn't do it for you; I did it for me." But that would be a lie, and I couldn't lie to Jack, because, have I mentioned those eyes? Besides, I couldn't lie to anyone, really. I was a bad liar, so I said something along the lines of, "Pshh, it was nothing."

"Just . . . you don't have to get yourself involved in my business, okay?"

"I didn't—" I said. But then I stopped, because like I said, I couldn't lie.

Jack noticed this, but he didn't push me. Rather, he shifted the topic of our conversation. "So . . . detention?" he asked, smiling. "You in detention? I thought pigs would fly before that happened."

That feeling came back, of me wanting people to think that I was a little badass. Being seen as a goody two-shoes had worked in my favor with the principal, but with Jack, it was different. I didn't want him to think of me that way. He went out with *Leanne*, for goodness' sake! I decided that detention was a good way to start easing into the whole badass thing.

"You don't know everything about me. I might be badder than you think," I said, mysteriously.

"Ha," Jack said.

I was embarrassed for sounding dumb, but Jack put his arm around me and said, "I didn't mean it as an insult. Just stay the way you are, okay?" We walked to detention together as he told me about the "joys" and "benefits" of detention.

When we got there, Jack greeted the rest of his detention pals and put on some show about how I was his hero for hitting Leanne. I was sure that many of Jack's detention buddies had had their "fragile" teenage boy hearts broken by Leanne, and they cheered and whooped. That's how I became instantly detention-popular. Jack made sure I was settled and comfortable, and then we all started talking about random things, like how much we hated the math teacher and how no one actually knew his last name. We laughed about everything from Tony's mood lighting—an inside joke among the whole town—to funny stories about how everyone else ended up in detention. Once the hour was over, Jack insisted on walking me home.

Friday's detention went by in the same way. On Saturday, I spent my day hunched over all of the homework that I regretted not doing in detention because I'd been too busy talking to Jack.

On Saturday night, Nicole practically dragged me out of my house so that I could be more social. When I got to her house, I realized that what she really wanted was for me to spill everything about what had been going on with Jack and me. I told her a little about math class and detention, but after ten minutes her face fell flat, and she said that I didn't tell her "anything of value."

Eventually, Jade came by, and I was relieved. We slept over at Nicole's, but Makenzie never showed up, despite Nicole calling her phone eight times and leaving seven voicemails urging her to be more social. Makenzie's excuse was that she was too busy doing homework for the three AP classes she decided to take sophomore year.

The next morning, I slept until noon. I walked into the living room with my hair still matted down and realized that Nicole and Jade had already been up for three hours. They'd gone through two sappy rom-coms while sharing a pint of ice cream in their pajamas. That was what we'd always done, but there was something about seeing them that morning that made me feel like the goody two-shoes I didn't want to be. I told them I had to go, which was a lie — I just didn't want Nicole to ask me any more annoying questions about Jack.

Once I got home, I checked my phone to see that I had an unread text. I couldn't help but smile when I saw who it was from. *Hey, it's Jack*, it read. *Do you want to go to Tony's after you're done with detention tomorrow?*

For the rest of the day, I lay on top of my bed, staring at the ceiling and thinking about how to respond. I felt kind of stupid when, at 7:00, all I texted him back was, *Yeah.*

The following week, things were very routine. When I saw Jack, or if I had a class with him, I'd say hi and he'd say hi back with a smile. My favorite part of the week was when Jack told me about the excuses he made to stay in detention with me.

On Monday it was "I thought school started at 8:15 instead of 8:00, whoops," so he got detention for an unexcused lateness. On Tuesday it was "The principal said I defaced school property because I drew a cartoon of the math teacher on my desk because he was boring me out of my mind." My favorite, though, was on Wednesday, when Jack said, "I accidentally started a food fight at lunch." It was kind of sweet that he did it all for me.

Wednesday was the last day of my detentions, and by that time I'd become really good friends with all of Jack's detention pals. We spewed inside jokes the entire time, and Jack's detention pals called us "the happily married couple." Like I said, that was Wednesday, Jack's favorite day of the week, since the creative writing club was on Wednesday. He sacrificed his highlight of the week for me, or at least that's what I thought.

When I was getting my jacket to go to Tony's, which had been our unspoken tradition by that time, despite the fact that it was unhealthy to have potato chips and pizza *that* consistently, Jack stopped me.

"We're going to the creative writing club," he said.

"*You're* going," I said. "Creative writing isn't my thing, remember?"

He ignored what I said, grabbed my arm, and dragged me to room 201. Before we walked in, he said, "Oh, and you're sharing today. No chickening out like last time."

As I opened my mouth to protest, he opened the door and pushed me inside. The members of the creative writing club were mostly made up of seniors, who looked up at us and shook their heads at each other as if to say "*sophomores*" disapprovingly.

Jack and I both took our seats. I looked for Cynthia, who had led the group last week, but she wasn't there. There was another senior girl leading the club that day who had big red glasses

27

that covered half of her face and stick-straight blond hair. She'd already written the prompt on the whiteboard: "Love."

Was the senior club leader girl serious? I did not want to write about love with my crush sitting right next to me. I looked over at Jack, who seemed kind of stuck too, but then he started to write. I opened my computer and was kind of curious to see what Jack was writing, so I looked over at his notebook while pretending to retie my hair, all while trying to make it seem like I wasn't looking. His handwriting was equivalent to chicken scratch, and I couldn't read a word, so I just sat there. I watched the others with their heads bent over their notebooks, or typing away on their computers, like they all were so confident in what they had to say.

"Love." The word scared me. I put my hands on the keyboard and tried to describe the feeling. I didn't even realize I had been thinking all of the things I wrote down until they were there, on the screen of my laptop.

When our time was up, the senior asked who wanted to share first. Jack nudged me encouragingly, and I ignored him. We caught the senior girl's eye, though, and she nodded at me. Before I realized what I was doing, I began to read: "Love. I'm afraid of it, yet I think about it all the time. I'm afraid, because, well, have you ever heard of a broken heart?"

That got a few chuckles, and I felt a satisfying tingling sensation in my hand, so I continued, "My mom got engaged when she was four years older than I am now to her high school sweetheart—my dad—and I can't help but feel pressured sometimes, like I have a timeline that I'm supposed to follow but can't. I'm almost sixteen, and I've never been kissed. I barely have any guy friends, and I feel like I'm so far behind most people my age."

I stopped before I read the next part, suddenly aware of Jack sitting next to me, holding my hand underneath the desks. "I try to be a good judge of character, but I think that if my head is clouded with so many feelings, I might misjudge a guy, and he might not be as good as I think. I'm afraid I'll fall in love with the idea of falling in love, only to realize that I made a mistake of thinking of it as actual love." The room was quiet, so I started reading faster. "I get nervous talking to guys, so this person — 'the one,' let's call him — will have to be my best friend because somehow I don't get nervous or stutter when I talk to my best friends." Aware of Jack sitting next to me, holding on to every word, I picked up my speed as I read, "I'm afraid of divorce. I'm afraid of getting married too late. I'm afraid of 'the one' dying. But most of all, I'm afraid of ending up alone."

I looked up to see some response, but when there was nothing, I added, "Sorry for ranting." No one said anything else except for a junior guy who said, "Good job," which I ignored, because all I could think about were the judgy seniors and Jack, who took his hand away from mine and was listening to something that the senior leader girl was saying.

Somehow, just then, it occurred to me how many embarrassing things I had just revealed to Jack. I looked at him, and he turned to me, looking at me differently. He didn't give me a look I was afraid of, like the stares the judgy seniors gave us. I didn't know whether it was possible, but his pale blue eyes seemed to have gotten softer.

He looked like he was going to say something to me, and he had just started to open his mouth, but before he could say anything to me, he took his jacket along with his backpack and ran off within five seconds, without giving me the chance to stop him.

Within eight seconds, I grabbed my jacket and backpack, because I wasn't as fast as Jack, and I ran out of the room too. I looked around, but he was gone. I felt my eyes getting teary, because he had just made my biggest fear come true. For the first time since I'd hung out with Jack, I felt alone.

Three

That night I walked home in the thirty-five-degree weather. I didn't wear a jacket, because nothing could warm me up inside, so why bother? I wished it was colder, though, like thirty-two degrees. I wished it was cold enough to freeze my tears, cold enough to freeze water, cold enough to freeze the world, cold enough to freeze *my* world. When I got to my house, I didn't want to walk in. I didn't want to be warm inside, because my heart hurt and felt ice-cold.

I told myself that I'd stand outside until I couldn't feel anything anymore. That was my plan, until some random soccer mom who was in charge of the carpool that week dropped Henry off. He asked me if I was cold, and I said yes, and then he told me to come inside. I didn't have it in me to explain my complicated schoolgirl crush I had on Jack to a five-year-old, so I followed him inside. When we got home, my mom was preparing her famous homemade pizza, and I couldn't help but think eating pizza this regularly wasn't healthy. Either way, I lost my appetite sometime between Jack abandoning me and standing in the thirty-five-degree weather. I mumbled something to my mom about not being hungry and ran up the stairs, not in the mood for her to probe and prod me. I had a lot of homework that I had neglected to do in detention because I was too busy talking to Jack. At that point I regretted talking to Jack at all and wished that I never walked into room 201 to begin with, so I made a promise to myself to avoid Jack for real this time. It was only 5:30, but I was exhausted, so I curled up in my bed and went to sleep.

The next morning, I woke up to my alarm beeping. For the first time, I wished that my "friendship" with Jack had been a dream. I knew that it wasn't a dream, because dreams can't actually hurt you.

My second thought was that I hadn't done my homework. It didn't bother me as much as it would have the week before, but I still didn't want to get out of bed. My stomach hurt, and so did my head. But I couldn't let Jack win whatever stupid mind game he was trying to play. I had to show him that I was strong, because if he noticed that I wasn't in math class, he'd know that he had won and that I was weak. Truthfully, I was weak, but I didn't want him to think that, so I pushed myself out of bed and stared at my closet, which I considered an accomplishment.

I guess I was acting strange, because after staring at the closet for a while, my mom knocked on my door and asked, "Bella, are you okay?"

"Yeah, I'm fine," I said.

"So . . ." she said, perching herself on the edge of my bed. "You've been spending a lot of time after school with Jack Walker, right? I saw him walk you home a few times last week."

"I guess," I said, shrugging. This was the part where you'd think that she would be angry, but the exact opposite was the case.

"Good for you, Bells, making some new friends. Is he your boyfriend or something?"

"Boyfriend?" my dad asked, peeking his head into my room with a cup of coffee in his hand.

"Yeah, Jack and Bella are dating," my mom told him. This was how rumors got started, and my mom was usually at the center of them.

"Jack, as in Jack Walker? The only sophomore on the varsity basketball team? Way to go, Bella," my dad said, ecstatic.

I wasn't annoyed anymore. I was angry. On any other day I would tolerate them, and maybe even force a smile, but Jack had hurt me in a way no one else had since Leanne, and I certainly didn't want to talk about it, so I grabbed my backpack, which was conveniently leaning against the closet door frame, and pushed past my dad, yelling, "I am not dating Jack! This is why I don't tell you things. Mom, you just spread lies, and Dad, you're only happy if the topic has to do with sports and angry if it doesn't, so just leave me alone. I'm going to school!"

I walked down the stairs to the kitchen, to where my jacket was hanging. I put it on and walked out the door, but not before I heard Henry, with a mouthful of microwave waffle, ask me, "Is it pajama day?"

I looked down at myself to see that I was still wearing pajamas. I'd slept in just sweatpants and a T-shirt, and I didn't mind wearing that to school. Besides, I wasn't going to go back into my house, where my parents could talk about my "relationship" with Jack. That was the reason I was staring at my closet for so long. Maybe I'd see Jack at school that day and should be wearing something nicer. At the same time, Jack was the very reason that I had to run out of my room while wearing sweatpants and a T-shirt in the first place.

I got to school five minutes late, and there was no one in sight, except for Jack, who was waiting for me at my locker.

"Bella, hey," he said, his eyes pleading for forgiveness.

I pushed past him and pretended to be busy putting in my locker combination. I didn't want him to be sorry. In a way, it was easier to think that he was playing games with my mind than to believe that he was a nice guy who made a mistake. My life was fine before Jack.

"Bella, I'm sorry I left. Just say something."

"What's there to say?" I asked, looking into my locker, only to realize that I already had my books. "You hurt me."

"Oh, you mean yesterday," he said.

"'Oh, you mean yesterday,'" I said, mocking him.

"Bella, I made a mistake, but you did too."

I slammed the locker door for dramatic effect. "I know I did. I made a mistake when I walked into that stupid creative writing club and started talking to you," I said. I wanted him to feel even a little piece of how I felt the day before, when I'd told him everything about me. I had shared my vulnerabilities and fears with Jack, and then he left without bothering to say goodbye or even trying to come up with some pathetic excuse.

I walked away from him—and all of the trouble and pain he had caused me—toward my next class.

"Bella, it wasn't a mistake," Jack said. "Come back and we'll talk."

As much as I wanted everything to go back to being fun between us, at that point I didn't exactly trust him, so I continued walking to class. That was saying a lot, because I didn't enjoy history since Ms. Anderson caught me hitting Leanne. I didn't know if it was just in my head, but it seemed that Ms. Anderson looked at me differently after the incident and wanted to make my life miserable in her class. The worst part was that Jack knew all

33

about Ms. Anderson and the fact that I had her class first period on Thursdays, and he was just trying to give me a better option. By leaving Jack, I was leaving behind every good memory I shared with him. For a fraction of a moment, I felt some empathy for him as I turned away. He was standing alone in the hallway and looked confused about where to go next, but the feeling faded when I remembered that *he* had left me first.

I reluctantly walked into Ms. Anderson's class. Everyone's eyes turned to me, including Ms. Anderson's, which made being late ten times worse than it had to be. If this had happened a week ago, Ms. Anderson would have pretended that she didn't notice me coming in late, or, after class, she would have asked whether everything was okay. But the way Ms. Anderson glared at me was like seeing the eyes of a whole new teacher. She was one of those teachers whose bad side you didn't want to get on, and, unfortunately, I had just secured myself a permanent spot.

"Office," she said, immediately.

"What? But I—" I said. I honestly didn't know what I was going to say, but she interrupted me.

"Go fill out a disciplinary report and then go to detention after school," she said. I didn't like it when she spoke to me in a tone that was like yelling without actually yelling.

When I walked out of the room, I saw Leanne out of the corner of my eye sitting in the back row. Leanne was a back-row kid, just like Jack. I thought that she would stand up for me, but I was reminded that those days were long gone when she did nothing but kept her head down.

I walked into the office, hoping that detention wasn't going to become a regular thing. I noticed that there was a new office lady, who was very large. I could tell she was new because she smiled way too much for someone who worked at a school. "Are you Bella?" she asked.

"Yes."

"Emily—I mean, Ms. Anderson, called ahead. Let me just get you a disciplinary report."

I watched as she shuffled through her desk, which was funny because she had the desk of a neat freak, and yet she was messing it all up to look for a simple disciplinary report. The funniest part was that disciplinary reports were blue, and I could see them right in front of us, stacked on a higher part of her desk. I didn't want to be the nice girl who pointed that out to her, so I just waited until she figured it out herself.

"They're the blue ones, above you," a familiar voice said. I turned around to see Jack sitting on one of the chairs outside of the principal's office.

"What are you doing here?" I asked.

"Turns out that skipping class to tell someone something really important is called ditching. Who knew, right?" He smirked.

"Bye, Jack."

"You forgot to fill out the disciplinary report," a voice said. You'd think that it was the office lady because that was her job, but, no, it was Jack, who was sitting back in his chair smugly. He looked comfortable, as if the school's office was his second home.

I took the disciplinary report from the office lady, who looked busy reorganizing her desk. "Thanks," I said under my breath, ambiguous as to whom I was saying thanks to. I didn't want to give Jack any type of satisfaction.

"You're welcome," Jack said, too proudly. "Does this mean you'll be joining me in detention today?"

"Yes, unfortunately."

"Why are you being so mean to me?" Jack asked suddenly, as if he was clueless, which he couldn't have been. "I thought we were having fun."

When I finished filling out the disciplinary report, I handed it back to the office lady, who took it, confused as to what to do with it next. I turned to look Jack in the eyes. His eyes were blue and soft, so I looked at his nose—yes, his nose. "Like I said: bye, Jack," I said, walking out like the badass I always wanted to be.

"Bella, wait up."

I didn't wait. Just then, the principal came out of his office and asked for Jack. The principal mumbled something about how teenagers have no volume control because they're always using headphones.

When I walked back to class, I checked my watch to see that I had wasted only five minutes of class time in the office. I mentally prepared myself for the thirty-eight minutes in Ms. Anderson's class as the number one student on her most-hated list. When I walked in, everyone turned to me except for Ms. Anderson, who continued writing on the whiteboard as she explained what the Entente was.

I took my seat next to Jade. She was drawing a fairy queen in the margins of her notebook. In that moment, I was jealous of her. She knew exactly what she wanted to do with her life, and as long as she kept her grades up, she would get into some really cool visual arts program. She wasn't boy crazy, even though she had a boyfriend who lived in Florida. They'd met at an art camp last summer, and they FaceTimed a lot, but it wasn't like he was running through her mind constantly like Jack was with mine. They were happy. If anything, it was Jade and her boyfriend— whose name I didn't remember, because she didn't talk about him that much—who were the "happily married couple," not Jack and me.

The bell rang and knocked me out of my fantasy. I noticed that Jade had finished her fairy queen, and she looked beautiful. Her hair looked like it was blowing freely in the wind, and she wore a crown of flowers. I saw how much detail there was in every petal, and the flowers that flowed down the fairy queen's dress made her look as though she was a part of nature. I wished I could do that—make things come to life on paper—but the best I could manage in artistic expression was either drawing a stick figure with sunglasses or confessing my feelings through a jumble of words, only to have my crush walk away.

I was trying to get over that and failing. For the rest of the day, I saw little things that reminded me of Jack. In the hallway, I saw Jack talking to some of his detention pals. At lunch, I saw some seniors eating pizza that they ordered from Tony's. Next to them, I saw a freshman eating potato chips. I mean, what were the chances? Finally, I had the class that I had been dreading all day: math.

I got there early. When I walked in, I was the second student in the class. The first was Jack. I tried to pretend I'd forgotten something and had to leave, but he looked at me with those soft blue eyes that were so hard to resist. "C'mon, Bella, stay," he said.

For the first time that day, I didn't resist and gave in. I sat down in my seat two rows in front of him, but I didn't say anything. I simply stared at my watch and waited for the seconds to pass, which they did, slowly. Jack asked if we could talk, but I stayed focused on the faint sound of the second hand ticking by. In my imagination, I amplified the sound—*tick, tick, tick*—and by the time the bell rang, Jack had stopped talking.

When the math teacher started to get boring, I eventually drowned him out too. Usually, I was able to follow what he was saying, even through his thick accent, but that afternoon, I was totally lost as I stared at the equations he'd written. I pretended to take notes and turned my attention instead to the "Jack and Luke Show" that was happening behind me.

Luke wore the same gray hoodie he always wore. "Hey, did you see the new office lady? What happened to Ms. Alperstein?" he asked, setting the theme for the day's episode.

"I bet she ate her."

"Ms. Alperstein? That woman was smaller than my nine-year-old sister."

"Stop being an idiot. I'm talking about the new lady. She's probably, like, two hundred pounds."

I rolled my eyes. Right when Jack was starting to convince me that he wasn't just the stereotypical obnoxious basketball jock, he said something to prove that my assumptions about him were right all along. All of a sudden the lights went out, then back on, then back off, then back on.

Jack whispered, "I bet that's her now, saying SOS in Morse code. 'Help! Help! It's me, Ms. Alperstein!'"

Luke laughed quietly enough for the math teacher not to hear. The math teacher was looking up at the lights, which had stopped flickering, and mumbled something under his breath in Russian. Out of the corner of my eye I saw Luke biting his tongue, trying not to burst. I admit I was trying not to crack up too. That is, until I remembered that I was still mad at Jack, and I didn't want him to make me laugh anymore, especially with a mean joke.

I turned around and whispered, "You're such a jerk. That wasn't funny."

I know it came out sounding weak. I wanted instead to push back my chair, yell at Jack, and cause some loud commotion like I'd done in the hallway with Leanne. It would've made more of an impression. But in the past, I'd always prided myself on being friends only with the good and nice kids, so this side of me that wanted to make a scene because of something my friend had said felt unfamiliar. Anyway, the last thing I needed was *another* detention.

"Then why are you smiling?" Jack asked.

I hadn't even intended to go along with Jack's jokes. I told him to shut up, but it came out harsher than I thought it would. That cut the Jack and Luke Show short, so for the rest of class I sat in silence, trying to draw Jade's fairy queen. In the end, it looked like a stick figure with sunglasses and hair lit on fire. A few minutes before the bell rang, Luke tried to revive the show.

"Hey, dude, I think it might be hard for you to tell her now that she hates you," Luke said. Jack didn't respond.

Was he going to give me some decent excuse as to why he ran off? Doubtful. I couldn't think of anything else he'd have to tell me, though, and I wasn't going to hang around to ask. I had to go to detention, even if it was a flimsy excuse to run out of class.

When the bell rang, I shot up from my seat so fast that the contents of my backpack spilled onto the floor. I hadn't cleaned my backpack out ever, and it wasn't a pretty sight. Jack bent down to help while everyone else crowded through the door, trying to leave as quickly as possible. I tried to gather everything up as fast as I could, but I had to pick up old dog-eared math worksheets that had lived at the bottom of my backpack for two years while Jack chased after my colored pens that had rolled behind several chairs.

Before I knew it, Jack and I were alone. Two weeks ago, I would have been ecstatic, but at that moment, all I wanted was to get out of the situation. As soon as all of my stuff was in my backpack, I zipped it closed and put it on, saying a quick thanks before walking away. Then, I felt a gentle tug on my backpack, which pulled me back.

"Bella, just wait. I need to ask you something."

My mind was screaming at my body to move, but my heart, or what was left of it, overpowered my mind. Later, I'd call it one of my greatest weaknesses.

"I've been rehearsing this in my head for almost the past twenty-four hours, and I'm still not even sure how to say this." He took a breath. "So, before, when I was saying that you made a mistake, what I was trying to . . . what I'm saying is . . . why did you say those things?"

"What do you mean? You told me to share."

"No!" he said, louder than both of us expected him to. He shifted back to his normal volume. "Why do you think so low of yourself? I just didn't understand, because in the week that I've gotten to know you, I think you're really amazing and . . . I like you." He looked at me with his blue eyes, the softest they had ever been.

I had words floating somewhere in the back of my head, but they weren't forming quickly enough into a thought. I felt that the three words Jack had just said would change the course of my life forever. "I have detention," I said. I wasn't ready for that kind of change, at least not yet.

"Okay," he said. "Then I'll walk with you. But, first, tell me how you feel."

"I like you too, but—"

"There aren't any buts. You like me; I like you. Why can't we be together?"

"Because we're different," I said, reluctantly. For the first time all day, I became self-conscious that I was standing in the classroom in my pajamas. I didn't want to have to acknowledge how different Jack and I were, but who were we kidding?

"Haven't you ever heard of how opposites attract?"

"Yes, but I don't know your world," I said. "This isn't a movie where I just get to date the popular basketball star. It's a fantasy, and fantasies don't happen. That's the whole point."

"Give me one reason why your fantasy can't come true."

I didn't want to say it, but I had to. I had to say anything that would stop him, even if my heart was telling me no. "Leanne," I said quietly, but loud enough for him to hear.

He contemplated this and then said, "Give it a chance; give *us* a chance. Let's try this for a little, and if it doesn't work, I can guarantee you a full refund."

"That's not how you're supposed to talk about a relationship, Jack," I said, but then again, how much did I really know? Either way, I continued, "It's not like you're trying to sell me on some infomercial product."

He laughed but then became serious again. "I'm sorry; it's just that . . . how can I convince you? I want this, Bella. I want you."

Never did I think I'd hear those words come out of Jack Walker's mouth, but surprises seemed to be the pattern lately. I had to tell him the truth, the same truth I'd declared in the creative writing room, in front of the judgy seniors. "I'm afraid," I said.

"Can I kiss you?" Jack asked, as if he didn't hear what I'd said.

Looking back, I don't know whether I thought letting him kiss me would make everything better, but I let him lean in, and I let him push himself against me, and I let his lips touch mine. I gave up all of my control, because I leaned in too. I also pushed myself against him and pressed my lips against his. Time didn't stop like I thought it would, and fairy dust didn't fall out of the sky, but he was a good kisser. I could tell despite my lack of experience. Why was I so surprised? He was Jack Walker, after all.

When he broke away from me, I was disappointed that the moment was over. I also thought that maybe I was a bad kisser, but that didn't really appear to be the case. Jack looked at me with his blue eyes as soft as ever and said, "Now you're almost sixteen, and you *have* been kissed."

Four

Things were changing, and they were changing fast. I was surprised to realize that I actually liked it, because I'd never liked change. I didn't like going from middle school to high school. Even though my middle school experience had been a nightmare, it had still been familiar and in my comfort zone. When we got to high school, I didn't like it when Leanne ditched me for "the girls," but I was starting to understand the rush and the thrill that Leanne had, or at least what I imagined her to have.

It had been a month since Jack kissed me. It took some time for the people in his friend group to adjust to me, but to everyone's surprise, I was funny. I made the "tough" basketball players crack up. In a way, I got their stamp of approval. That was easy compared to the girls. They were the real tough ones, and even after a month of sitting at Jack's lunch table, I still couldn't make myself go over to them and get their identically glossed lips to form a smile. I told myself that I still had my old friends, but I didn't realize that referring to them as my *old* friends was already a bad sign.

I hadn't really thought about it until then, but the girls I called my old friends—Makenzie, Nicole, and Jade—had really been Leanne's friends until she ditched them too. Up until we first started middle school, it had always been just Leanne and me, me and Leanne. I thought she was all I needed, but Leanne convinced me that we needed to be more social and make more friends, and I reluctantly agreed. Leanne was the glue that held the five of us together. When we got to high school and she started dating Jack, I became closer with the other girls, but I couldn't call any of them my true best friend. I couldn't fill the void with anyone but Leanne, so since I'd started hanging out with Jack's friends, I didn't feel too awful that I didn't miss Makenzie, Nicole, and Jade that much. Yes, I missed talking to other girls, but I was having fun.

Before I started talking to Jack, I'd never spoken to a boy except to say something stupidly polite like excuse me. The only other time I talked to boys was when they assumed I was smart and they asked me to give them answers to homework or to help them cheat on a test. I said no, obviously; I was smart enough to do that. Anyway, I was becoming a different person, and I liked it. Instead of asking me for homework answers, boys asked if I was coming to the basketball game that night, and instead of asking for help to cheat on a test, they asked me to help bring over some pizza from Tony's for pre-game pep rallies.

I always stayed close to Jack, though. It still felt a little awkward when I was around his friends and he wasn't. We always sat together at lunch. One Friday, Jack was waiting for me in the cafeteria with two trays of food, one for him and one for me. There was a pizza bagel and chips on one tray that Jack was holding, and I smiled to myself, because I couldn't handle how lucky I was to have a sweet boyfriend like him.

We walked over to his friends, but instead of putting my tray down next to his on the table like he did every other day, he handed my tray to me. I gave him a puzzled look, and he nodded at the table next to ours where the girls sat. Why was everyone always trying to convince me to be more social? I mean, why couldn't they pick on super social people for once and tell them to be more quiet? I tried to give Jack a pleading look with cute doe eyes, but he just shook his head, put his tray on the table, and then put his backpack on the seat that would have otherwise been mine.

I looked over to the girls. Saying that Beatrix was the queen bee of our grade would have been an understatement. She was that girl you thought existed only in movies, where every girl aspired to be like her and saw her as the image of coolness. Back when Leanne and I were best friends—before she and Beatrix became "besties" for a year and before Leanne became the sopho- more slut—we called her Queen *Bee-atch*-rix. That was our secret name for her, though. It didn't work as well anymore because by sophomore year, Beatrix liked to go by Bea. By then, it didn't matter because Leanne and I were way past secret nicknames.

Bea gave me an unfriendly wave that no one could master quite like a Queen Bee-atch. I went to sit down at the table with Bea and three of the other girls, who I couldn't help but think either envied me or hated me.

At first, I picked at my pizza bagel and didn't say much. Bea was telling a story about picking out a dress at the designer bou- tique in town, and the girls were hanging on to her every word. They chimed in about what they would be wearing, until Bea interrupted them and turned to me. "Oh yeah, Bella," Bea said. "I assume you're coming to my party Saturday night because you're Jack's . . . friend?" Envy.

"Girlfriend," I corrected her, realizing that I had the one thing she wanted but couldn't have—Jack. He had mentioned how they were all going to Bea's sweet sixteen that weekend, and after some convincing, I said I'd be up for it.

"Right, right," she said distantly. "Let's not fixate on the details. Anyway, it's a little last-minute, but I'm throwing a little pre–sweet sixteen get together for the girls tonight. Do you want to tag along?"

"What are you going to do?" I asked. If they were going to give each other mani-pedis, swap clothes, and gossip, I could think of at least a hundred other things I'd rather be doing.

"Well, first we're getting Italian."

My face lit up. "At Tony's?"

"Oh, God no. We're going to L'Italiano, then to La Crèmerie, and then the girls will come over for the night. We're going to have a marathon of my favorite show, *Gossip Girl.*"

It was such classic Queen Bee-atch-rix style to go to the fancy Italian restaurant and then to the ice cream parlor where it cost fifteen dollars for half a scoop of ice cream—and that's without toppings. Of course, her favorite show would be *Gossip Girl,* because what else could portray her personality so well?

When I realized that she was waiting for an answer, I said the first thing that popped into my head: "So, it's like a sleepover?"

Bea scoffed, "Sleepover? What are we, five?"

"Of course not," I said. "I'd love to come to your not-sleepover."

Bea put on the fakest smile I'd ever seen. What else could I expect from a girl like that?

For the rest of lunch, Bea ignored me, and I sat in silence, listening to the girls gossip. I learned a couple of things: one of the girls, Heather, said Luke and Leanne hooked up for the fourth time at some random party. I looked over to Luke sitting at Jack's table, who winked at me like what he had with Leanne was nothing. I shuddered in disgust. I could never be in a relationship like that with no strings attached. That's why I liked Jack. He was the embodiment of commitment—at least to the extent of a high school romance. Then, another one of the girls, Mila, chimed in and said that someone saw a mystery man drive our guidance counselor to school and saw them make out. On any other day that would have amused me, but I was still thinking about Leanne.

When the bell rang, the girls disbanded and headed to class. Grace, the last of the girls, stayed behind, slowly gathering her things. Grace had been the quietest person at the table, even quieter than me. I had always thought that Grace was nice, and I didn't understand why she was one of the girls, except I kind of did know. Grace was stunning, with jet-black hair and piercing green eyes. She was by far the prettiest girl in school, even prettier than Bea, who would never admit it out loud. Grace was the new girl at school that year, and Bea knew to take her into the fold right away. As the saying goes, "Keep your friends close and your enemies closer."

Grace and I just happened to have class together anyway, right after lunch, so we walked to chemistry together. She told me that once I got to know Bea, she wasn't so bad. I just nodded along, hoping she was right. To my relief, when we got to class, we had a substitute teacher. Someone said that the chem teacher was visiting his sister who just had a baby. I was happy for him, but even more happy that I didn't have to spend fifty minutes mixing fluids with the lab set while having no idea what I was doing.

I ended up talking to Grace for the whole period. I didn't know why it hadn't occurred to me to not hang out with her before, because I found that she was one of those rare genuinely nice people without ulterior motives. We talked about everything from how she was from Cleveland—or Chicago, I couldn't remember which—to the cute puppy she got last spring, to deciphering something her boyfriend said over FaceTime the night before. She said that she was dating her childhood sweetheart from home and they were really good at keeping up the long-distance thing. "I know what a lot of people think of me," she said, keeping her green eyes down. "That I'm too quiet and pathetic for holding on to a middle school relationship."

"No! I think it's romantic," I said. I couldn't help but think that maybe Grace would be the person to fill my Leanne-shaped void. But I was getting ahead of myself. We'd had two conversations up to that point.

"You don't think it's pathetic to hold on?" she asked.

Grace was opening up to me, and I felt like I needed to say something to open up to her too, so I told her one of my secrets I'd never told anyone before. "I liked Jack for a long time," I said. "Even before Leanne—my ex-best friend—started going out with him. I think she knew that I liked him too. Anyway, now Jack and I are together and happy, so you never know what can happen if you stay patient and hold on."

Grace's face twisted up for a second before she smoothed out her expression again and smiled. I wondered whether I'd said too much. "It must be hard, though, doing the long-distance thing," I said.

The bell rang, and we reluctantly said goodbye and exchanged phone numbers. Grace caught a glimpse of my home screen. I hadn't bothered to change it since the summer, but maybe it was because I didn't want to. It was a picture of my cousins and me posing in front of the Statue of Liberty, and I was laughing at the fact that it was their first time there despite the fact that they had lived in New York City all of their lives. I never loved getting my picture taken, but that picture had somehow captured every feeling.

"Wow, that's an amazing picture, Bella. You look beautiful there."

"Thanks," I said. My appreciation for Grace's genuine kindness grew. "I'll see you around."

"Definitely," Grace said. I was excited because I hadn't made a new girl friend in years.

That night, as I was getting ready for Bea's get-together, the doorbell rang early. Grace had texted that she would pick me up at 7:00 to walk over to Bea's house, but I checked my phone to see that it was only 6:30. My mom opened the door, and I heard her voice float up the stairs, greeting someone with a familiar, happy tone. My mom, of course, was beyond ecstatic that I was going to Bea's pre–sweet sixteen get-together.

Thirty seconds later, Nicole appeared in my bedroom's doorway.

She scanned my outfit. "That's a little fancy, but we don't have time; we've gotta go. Jade's mom is waiting for us in the car," she said.

"Huh?" I said, more confused than I should have been.

"Jade's sixteenth birthday," Nicole said, spinning her hand in a circle as if that would churn up my memory. "We're going to the art gallery in the city that she's been dying to go to. We've been planning this for weeks, remember?"

"Right, the thing is—" I started. For one second, I thought about telling her the truth, but then I blurted out, "I can't. I'm not feeling well. My mom wanted me to try on this dress, but after that I was going to put on sweats and go to bed."

"But it's Jade's birthday," Nicole said.

I didn't understand how I could've forgotten. Jade and Bea had the same birthday, which was the next day. I had been there every year when Jade had tried to plan birthday parties, only to have no one show up because Bea always threw a party on the same day. Eventually, Jade gave up and kept things small. I knew that I was letting her down, but I continued with my story.

"I'm sorry, Nicole. I took my temperature, and it's like a hundred degrees. I'm just not feeling well. I'm sorry."

"Bella, I know you've been busy with Jack and hanging out with all of his friends, but — "

"I swear it has nothing to do with them, " I said.

"Well, I hope you feel better," Nicole said, convinced. "We'll come by tomorrow to tell you about it."

"Can't wait," I said, weakly. I added in a cough, for good measure, and grabbed some sweatpants from my closet as Nicole was leaving.

When she was gone, I threw the sweatpants on the ground like they were infested with disease. My mom came by my room and said, "Where's Nicole going?"

"Come on, Mom," I said. "Nicole isn't invited." I played with my hair, debating on whether to leave it down or put it up.

Five

I was a part of something. I was finally a part of something. After all the years of saying that I didn't want to be friends with the girls—despite my mom's many pleas—I was friends with them, and I liked it, but I'm getting ahead of myself.

I was sitting in the limo Bea had ordered to drive into the city. The girls were gossiping about pretty much everything, and it was clear that their favorite topic was Leanne. It was more like Bea's favorite topic, which meant it was everyone else's too. I didn't want to talk about Leanne behind her back; I didn't want to talk about anyone behind their back. That was something Jade always honored—she never gossiped, and I always admired that about her. If I was going to be pulled into being one of the girls, I wanted to be as gossip-free as possible, so I stayed as quiet as Grace. Unfortunately for me, Bea wouldn't stand for it, because I wasn't as pretty as Grace, who Bea needed to keep somewhat happy so that she wouldn't become a threat. At least that's how I thought Bea's mind worked.

"So, Bella, you and Leanne used to be best friends, right?" Bea asked. I nodded to avoid talking as much as possible. "Anything you wanna tell us about that *slut*?" she asked.

I shuddered at that last word, and even though everyone had been calling Leanne that for months now, I couldn't help but feel bad every time I heard it. I thought about how Bea and Leanne had been best friends too, even more recently than Leanne and me, and yet Bea could call her a name without feeling anything.

In a second attempt to avoid talking, I shook my head. What I was really telling her though was, *No, I don't have any dirt on my ex-best friend. Why do you want to know so much about her anyway? You two were best friends last year, remember? Or can you not be associated with someone you're now calling the sophomore slut? Is it bad for your image?* I'm pretty sure that all Bea got from my expression was the simple no. I turned away, wanting her to move on to another girl, urging *her* to gossip, not *me*. Mila spoke up and said she had some encounter with Leanne in the lunchroom, when Heather turned to me and asked, "Tell us what we're all dying to know. What's Jack like?"

Heather was just like Nicole, the boy-crazy one with a never-ending list of questions.

I wished that Bea would ignore her and ask me another yes or no question, because I couldn't nod or shake my head to one of Heather's open-ended questions that actually required me to talk. All eyes turned to me, and Bea just stared with her face frozen into a smirk.

"Good," I said, pretending like it was more of a "How is he doing?" question, rather than what they really wanted to know.

"C'mon," Heather said, relentlessly. "Spill."

I looked around the car trying to find a way out of the conversation. I made eye contact with Bea, whose eyes were shining, cold, and jealous. I was stealing her spotlight, the attention that she always had, and she wanted it back. What she didn't understand was how I didn't care about being in the spotlight, and I was going to use that to my advantage.

"Do you wanna hear about how we met? Or how we started to—" I didn't really know how to end the sentence, but the girls understood, and they all leaned in without speaking. Then Bea made a show of yawning, which we all chose to ignore.

In that moment something came over me. It became my mission to make Bea as jealous as possible. I told the girls what they wanted to hear. They just sucked it up, and I could tell that they were also starting to like me more and more. But why did that make me feel like I was some kind of villain, leading them into a trap?

Bea let out a loud sigh of relief when the limo stopped in front of L'Italiano. The sign was warmly lit and had a picture of a bright poppy. People on the street walked past the restaurant doors as if they had somewhere they needed to be five minutes ago. For a moment, I was thankful to have a reason to stop talking. It seemed that, at the same time, everyone else remembered how the night was supposed to be about Bea, not me. The girls switched their attention back over to Bea and crowded around her as we walked out of the limo and into the restaurant.

Grace hung back with me and said, "They're really starting to warm up to you, you know?"

"Oh, I know," I said, then realized I might have come off as conceited.

To my surprise, Grace said, "It's about time someone threw that queen off her throne."

"What happened to her 'not being so bad'?"

"Things change. Besides, I was trying to convince myself more than I was trying to convince you."

I told her about the nickname Leanne and I had come up with—Queen Bee-atch-rix. Grace cracked up, and I laughed with her.

After that, we sat down at the table with the rest of the girls. I took a moment to process the restaurant with its dim lighting and expensive-looking paintings hanging all around us, before I turned my attention back to Grace. We ignored Bea and talked to each other about how we both didn't know what was going on in chem. Then Heather joined in on our conversation, and we started talking about the make-out session between the guidance counselor and her new boyfriend. Then Mila joined in on the conversation, and it became clear that I was the life of the party. Bea turned her attention to her phone, pretending to be amused so that someone would ask her what she was looking at. No one did, and the best part of it all was that I wasn't even trying.

I turned my attention back to the conversation. Heather asked, "Is being a guidance counselor a real job anyway? What are they guiding?"

I laughed along with everyone else and turned my attention to the front of the restaurant, where Jade, Nicole, and Makenzie—who never went out on Friday nights, because she was always too busy studying—had just walked in. I snapped my attention toward the three of them to make sure that my eyes weren't betraying me. Thankfully, my old friends were too busy talking to the hostess to notice me staring. But one thing was clear; I was in big trouble.

"I have to go," I said. The girls stared at me. Bea put her phone in her purse. "To where?" she said. It took me a couple seconds to realize that I had nowhere *to* go. We were in the city, which meant we were over an hour away from home, and that was only if traffic wasn't too bad. After a long pause, I ended my sentence by adding, "To the bathroom."

"Don't be such a dweeb about announcing it," Bea said, smiling at the chance of gaining back the attention of the girls.

I didn't want to give her the pleasure of seeing me embarrassed, so I got up from the table as fast as I could. As I walked across the restaurant, I heard someone call out my name. It was Jade, but I pretended like I didn't hear her and kept walking. I couldn't bear to see the very hurt look I knew would be on her face.

In the bathroom, I darted into the first stall. If I knew my old friends like I thought I did, Makenzie would be in the bathroom at any second, ready to pound my face like a volleyball. Did I mention that aside from being ultra-competitive with grades, she was also the most aggressive player on the volleyball team? It turned out that I did know Makenzie very well, because within seconds, I heard her push open the bathroom door as hard as she could.

"Bella, come out," Makenzie said. She hesitated for a minute, probably debating whether she should beat me up. "I know you're in here. I'm not an idiot—4.0 GPA, remember?" Makenzie brought that up whenever possible, and it was oddly comforting to hear her do it in that strange bathroom we'd both never been in. Then I remembered how she was probably going to pound my face like a volleyball. "Bella, get out right now!" Makenzie yelled, and I never liked messing with her, so I slowly walked out of the stall. "You don't have to be scared of me," she said.

That was a relief, and when I let out a big, exaggerated sigh, I got a chuckle out of Makenzie, which was usually hard to do. Then she put her serious face back on, and I knew this wasn't the time for fun and games, so I just said, "Okay."

"All I want to say is that if you want to be friends with the girls, and Jack, and whoever else you're hanging out with these days, go ahead. I'm fine with that. Just tell me the truth and don't lie to me, or Nicole, or Jade, and be so God-awful about it, because that was a really mean thing you did."

"Okay," I said. I'd never heard Makenzie talk like that before. She was usually so intense that hearing her hurt was a surprise.

"Good," Makenzie said, nodding. "So is it us or them?"

Had I missed something? Was she really making me choose right then and there? I hated to admit it, but the decision was a lot easier than it should have been. It was between my old friends, whom I'd never really clicked with, and my new friend Grace, which came with the opportunity to throw Queen Bee-atch-rix off her throne and steal her crown. "I'm sorry, Makenzie," I said, and that was it.

She walked out. She didn't pound my face like a volleyball, but I still felt bad and guilty.

Once I finally gathered myself enough to walk out of the bathroom, my old friends were gone. I had a feeling that they'd be gone from my life for a while, but when I saw Bea's smug face with the spotlight on her again, I completely forgot about the drama between my old friends. The hurt, the guilt, all of it. When I reached the table, Bea's eyes flickered toward me, and her smug expression changed instantly into a frown. I was the clear cause of her misery, and I couldn't be happier.

For the rest of dinner, the girls kept asking me questions about Jack, and I kept giving them answers. As we left the restaurant, Bea tried to ask me something unrelated, but she got shushed, and I felt a rush of power sweep through my entire body.

We got to La Crèmerie just as they were about to close. Bea dropped some names, because her dad supposedly had friends in high places, and the employee let us in. Bea let Grace order first, because she needed more time to decide. When it was time to pay, Grace took out her wallet and fished for some cash. Bea had finally decided what flavor she wanted, and she crossed her arms as she waited for Grace.

"Why can't you frickin' pay already? How hard is it to find fifteen dollars?" Bea said.

Grace plucked out her last twenty from her wallet and gave it to the cashier. After a loud scoff, Bea ordered. The line moved quickly after that. None of the flavors with their hard-to-pronounce names looked appealing to me, so when it was my turn, I played it safe and ordered vanilla.

"Vanilla, seriously?" Bea asked. "We came all the way to La Crèmerie, and all you order is frickin' vanilla?"

Leanne and I used to joke about how Bea had ears everywhere.

The old me would have listened to Bea and ordered something different, but the new me wasn't going to take any of her crap. I paid for my overpriced half scoop of vanilla ice cream and stepped to the side.

The ice cream came in a ruffled cup. I tasted a spoonful. It was really good. It was more than that—it was the type of good that's indescribable, the kind where there are no words to express how good it was. It was so good that it almost stopped me from doing what I was about to do.

Bea was talking to Heather and too busy to notice me plant myself in the perfect spot to "accidentally" dump my half scoop of indescribably good vanilla ice cream on her expensive-looking black shirt. I waited for the perfect moment to just tip the cup . . . but then Grace tapped me on the shoulder. As I turned to her, Bea walked away to talk to Mila.

"How's your vanilla?" Grace asked.

"It's good," I said, with only half of my attention committed to the conversation. Maybe it was a good thing that I didn't "accidentally" get ice cream all over Bea's shirt. Maybe it was a sign that I was in over my head to think that all of the girls would choose me over their Queen Bee-atch-rix after *really* only talking to me for one night.

"Mine's awful." Grace stuck out her tongue. "I can't even pronounce its name. I wish we had just gotten pints of Ben and Jerry's—not that any of the girls would actually eat a pint of ice cream."

"Oh my God, yes," I said. "Nothing beats sitting in your pajamas, watching TV, and eating a pint of Ben and Jerry's."

"Queen Bee-atch-rix doesn't realize that everything doesn't have to be perfect," Grace said with a devilish grin, as if she liked the way Bea's nickname sounded on her tongue.

"Exactly." Where had this girl been all my life? I hadn't gotten along with a girl this well since . . . Leanne.

For the rest of the night, Grace and I talked and laughed, but mostly we laughed all of the way back to East Shore, where the limo dropped us off at Bea's house. Bea lived in a mansion, and even calling it that would be an understatement. When we arrived, she led us to her room to watch *Gossip Girl*. I'd never watched the show before, but I picked up pretty quickly that it was about a group of rich kids. The main characters were these two best friends, Serena and Blair, who fought way too much for being best friends. For the most part, everyone was in a relationship with everyone at some point.

As we watched the show, Grace kept commenting on everyone's outfits. I'd never really been into fashion, so I kept quiet. Maybe I'd had some childhood trauma from all the times my mom dragged me along on her endless shopping sprees, but that's just one theory.

"I love how you can use fashion to be anyone you want," Grace said. "It's like your clothes are your identity. When you walk into a room, one of the first impressions people have about you is from your clothes. Does that not fascinate you?"

Grace had a point. I'd never thought of it that way. I'd never thought about fashion much, considering the fact that I had always been a sweatshirt-and-jeans kind of girl. I usually avoided conversations about things like two-hundred-dollar boots that were on sale.

What stuck with me about what Grace said was how clothes could allow you to be whomever you wanted. There were countless times when I wanted to become a different person. That feeling started when I'd played dress-up as a four-year-old and then grew in middle school and high school when, as pathetic as it sounded, I wished I was pretty enough to have a boyfriend like Leanne or rich enough to be popular like Bea.

"Hello? Earth to Bella." Grace waved her hand in front of my face. "What do you think?"

At that point, I'd forgotten what her question was. Grace shrugged and shook her head. Then I remembered that she had asked for my opinion, and it turned out that I actually had a lot to say. But if I'd learned anything during the past two months, it was that saying anything else after my long pause would have been awkward.

I stayed quiet and started to *actually* pay attention to the Serena-and-Blair drama. Bea kept munching on her special diet popcorn, which was the noisiest food I'd ever heard, but I managed to zone that out as I was taken into the "scandalous lives of Manhattan's most elite."

I didn't realize how appreciative I should have been of the *Gossip Girl* marathon until it was too late. At some point around 2:00 a.m., Bea turned off the TV. I thought that meant we would go to sleep, but I'd never been to a Queen Bee-atch-rix sleepover before, and it turned out that sleeping was not going to be a part of it.

Bea announced that we were going to play an epic game of truth or dare. My stomach sank. I hated truth or dare. I wasn't the daring type, and I definitely wasn't the type to expose myself by telling all of my secrets to people I'd started talking to only the day before.

With my old friends, I'd always managed to evade the game with some lame excuse like "I'm tired," and they wouldn't make me play. Sometimes, when they would play and I wouldn't, I'd feel guilty that they were exposing themselves and sharing their deepest, darkest secrets, while I wasn't telling them anything. Then, that guilt would subside when I thought about having to *actually* say something secretive about myself. The last and only person I'd told my deepest, darkest secrets to was Jack that first night, and I didn't want the list to get any bigger.

"I'm tired," I told Bea.

She shot me back a look that was more appalled than offended.

"Buzzkill," she said in a loud voice.

"Excuse me?"

"You didn't have to come to my party, and you're clearly not my biggest fan. But you chose to be here. So I'd appreciate it if you'd suck up your feelings and try to have fun. If you can't do that, then the least you could do is pretend, okay?"

I felt some respect for Bea. She was genuine, honest, and a girl who didn't take anyone's crap—even though, in this instance, it was my crap we were talking about. Was it possible that Bea wasn't really a bee-atch?

I ended up playing truth or dare and had fun. When I played, I wasn't the old goody two-shoes Bella—I was Jack's girlfriend Bella, which was who the girls wanted me to be anyway. I felt more daring, and when it was my turn, I always picked dare. That meant I didn't have to expose my secrets like I had been afraid of doing, and the fear I had surrounding the game disappeared. I had fun, and it wasn't the fake kind. Was it possible the girls weren't so bad?

That night, they hadn't been anything but nice to me. And then there was Bea, who maybe wasn't the Queen Bee-atch I had made her out to be. It made me wonder whether I had been living through high school—or my entire life, even—the wrong way. Maybe I held on to the appearance of things for too long. With these hazy thoughts, I started falling asleep, and for the first time, I was actually excited to celebrate Bea's sweet sixteen the next day.

Six

The next morning, I woke up to the sound of hurling. Not the type of "throwing a ball" hurling. I mean real "throwing up" hurling. I looked at Bea's alarm clock to see that it was 11:54. I'd never been the type of person to sleep late. I was that weird teenage girl who actually enjoyed waking up early and getting a head start on the day. It may have had something to do with my five-year-old brother, who on weekends would wake up at the crack of dawn and jump on my bed until I woke up to make him his favorite breakfast, microwave waffles. My parents, on the other hand, could somehow sleep into the afternoon, even with us banging bowls and pans in the kitchen.

After a minute of looking around and listening to Mila and Heather talking, I learned that one of the flavors had bad cookie dough in it, which led to Bea and Grace getting food poisoning. It was karma. Although Grace was nice and she had gotten sick too. She already went home. So maybe it wasn't karma—just caramel—because it was the ice cream after all.

The room started to smell sour. I got out of bed and stuffed all of my things into my bag. As I zipped it up, my phone buzzed from somewhere in the sheets. I could name a whole list of people I hoped weren't calling (Makenzie, Jade, Nicole), because I wasn't ready to face them after last night. When I finally found my phone tangled up in the sheets, I saw that it was Jack.

I hadn't thought about Jack in hours, which was record-breaking. I couldn't think of the last time I hadn't thought about him constantly. I never wanted to be that girl with the boyfriend who took up all of her thoughts, her dreams, her actions, everything, really. I had to remember how to be my own person. I stared at the call and let it go to voicemail.

A minute later, Jack's voicemail popped up on my phone. He was one of those rare people who actually took the time to leave a voicemail, unlike most people I knew. I didn't listen to it right away, because I wasn't going to let him dominate my life, like I had always thought he had done with Leanne. I grabbed my bag and didn't even bother changing clothes. I thought that if I stayed even a second longer, I might throw up too, from the smell in the room.

Mila and Heather went downstairs but left their stuff behind, so they weren't planning on leaving yet. I almost didn't bother thanking Bea. As I was leaving her bedroom, though, I thought better of it. It was only the night before when I thought that maybe we could be friends, just maybe. And she had gotten sick on her birthday, which is a downer for anyone. I put my stuff down and walked across the room to knock on the bathroom door.

Bea's bathroom had a sliding door that separated the toilet from the rest of the bathroom. The bathroom was pretty spacious; it even had room for a cushioned seat, which I sat on as I held my nose. When Bea slowly opened the sliding door and saw me, she looked up with tired eyes. It was funny; I'd never seen Bea look tired. Even early this morning at 4:00 a.m., she had the energy of a little kid on a sugar high.

"Thanks for having me," I said.

Bea crawled out toward me. Her dirty blond hair was tied up in a messy bun, and she wore a bathrobe. She closed the small door behind her. With a raspy voice, she said, "I hope you're happy."

"What do you mean?" I asked. "I'm not the reason you got food poisoning."

Bea laughed, a happy laugh. She was full of surprises that morning. "You should have seen your eyes. I meant about the vanilla ice cream. That's their best flavor."

"What? But I thought you said —"

"Shh, just don't tell anyone, okay?"

"Okay?" I said.

"Oh, and you'll be happy to know that I canceled my party today."

"Because you're sick?"

"Don't worry about me, Bella. Anyway, I know you're not big on partying."

"I was kind of excited, actually," I said.

Bea smiled, surprised.

"You know, you're not as bad as I thought you were," I said.

Bea frowned in the way that was similar to her face at school. Her Queen Bee-atch-rix voice came back, and she asked, "What do you mean, I'm 'not as bad as you thought'?"

I said goodbye and ran.

When I got home, the sun was out, and the light was warm, so I stood on the porch steps to listen to Jack's voicemail: "Hey, Bella, I heard Bea's party was canceled. Thanks for hanging out with her, by the way. So I'm calling to see if you wanted to do something else tonight. We could go to Tony's, or watch a movie, or do something else. Bye, love you . . . oh, shoot. Hey, Mom, do you know how to cancel a voicemai—"

I played the voicemail five more times just to make sure that he had said "love you." Was it more of an instinctual "love you," like when you call a relative and sign off by saying "love you"? Did he really mean to say it? And if he did, then why did he say "oh, shoot" at the end?

By the time I stopped replaying the voicemail, I realized I had also missed ten text messages from Jack that basically all said not to listen to the voicemail. In the last text, he asked if I still wanted to go out with him that night because Bea's party was canceled.

If Jack had sent ten texts asking me not to listen to his voicemail, then he probably didn't mean what he said. But another voice in my head said that Jack did mean it and he wanted to tell me in person that night. Maybe that voice came from the overly romantic part of me that had fantasized about Jack over the past few years without ever expecting the fantasy to become reality. Still, I could hope. I sent a text and said we should go to Tony's. Despite my unhealthy intake of pizza lately, I thought that if he was going to say that he loved me, I wanted it to be romantic, in the place where we'd gone on our first date. Within seconds, Jack texted back: *Great. I'll pick you up at 6:00.*

I noticed that Jack always used proper punctuation and no shortcuts when he texted. There Jack was, occupying all my thoughts once again. But I felt like I loved him too. Even though all of the movies and TV shows and books I'd consumed in my lifetime up to that point told me that a month was way too early to say "I love you," I really felt that I'd fallen in love with Jack. He was perfect and so much more. If he wasn't going to tell me he loved me that night, then maybe I could build up enough courage to say that I loved him. And if I was being *really* honest with myself, I'd already been in love with the fantasy of him for years.

It was 6:00, and I had been staring at the time on my phone for hours because I had nothing better to do. It wasn't until 5:45 that I realized that I had an English essay due in two days, but I told myself to screw it, because two days still meant that I had another day. Besides, I'd rather hang out with Jack than do some stupid English paper. By the time Jack rang my doorbell, five minutes after 6:00, I became somehow fixated on the guilt of not working on my English essay. My grades were slipping, and I'd dealt with it by not looking at the growing list of late assignments online. How could I care so much about my classes when there was Jack, the pre-game pep rallies, the girls and Bea, and my mom and dad, who were so excited about these new parts of my life while they never seemed to care about the rest?

I opened the front door. Seeing Jack wiped away the worries I had about my grades, and I remembered what he had said to me: "Bye, love you."

I let the memory of those words play on repeat in my head as we walked out of my house, down my street, and to Tony's. When we got there, I realized that neither of us had actually said anything. We ordered as usual, and I told him I'd pay and that he should go grab a seat.

Other than that, I stayed quiet, because I didn't want to give him a reason to bring up the voicemail and tell me that he didn't mean what he said. After hours of staring at my phone, I'd decided that I would tell him boldly, before he could take back what he had said—I love you, Jack. But here we were together, in reality, and I wasn't ready to make myself vulnerable.

I met Jack at our table with two slices of pizza and two bags of potato chips. I'd forgotten the waters. "You heard the voice-mail didn't you?" he asked.

"What makes you say that?" I asked, sitting down.

"Bella, I know you're lying, so I'm assuming you heard what I said to you."

"That Bea's party was canceled?" I asked, trying to veer the conversation in a different direction.

"You know what I'm talking about. At the end?"

"Oh, *that*."

"Yeah, *that*. About that—"

The tone in his voice told me that he didn't mean those words after all. I was crushed, and I cut him off. "Look, Jack, I know you didn't mean it and it was just a mistake. We can forget about it and just move on, okay?"

"That's not what I was going to say."

I wondered if he was going to break up with me. It would make sense that he'd let *me* choose where we were going for once, so he could let me down easy. I wondered whether he could really be that messed up.

Then, Jack took my hand and said, "Bella, I know this is fast, and I wasn't planning on telling you this. Hell, I didn't even realize it, but I've done a lot of thinking today, and I realized I love you. I don't know why I didn't try to get to know you before, and it's crazy, because I've known you for years without really getting to know you. I regret that, because you're full of surprises and a truly amazing person. So, yes, Bella I-don't-know-your-middle-name Carter, I love you."

There was the thing with Jack saying my name that I loved so much. I wanted to tell him that my middle name was Riley, but most of all, I wanted to tell him that I loved him too. I opened my mouth and said, "I haven't started my English essay."

We both just sat there, confused. By the look on Jack's face, I had ruined the best scene of a romance novel, because what girl says "I haven't started my English essay" when the love of her life says that he loves her too? Me, only me.

"Do you, um, want help with your English essay?" Jack asked.

"Yeah, I guess," I said. What I really wanted was for Jack to say that he wanted me to say that I loved him back. I didn't have enough courage to tell him that on my own. I wanted him to forget about my stupid English essay, and I wanted to play him saying that he loved me on repeat in my head.

Maybe we could redo the moment. As Jack shuffled through the backpack that he always carried around with him, I said, "I love you too," but too quietly for him hear. I was trying to convince myself that I could somehow work my response into the conversation, but it didn't happen.

He took out his beat-up notebook. I began thinking of how Jack was a writer. He most likely got As on all of his papers, so maybe he could actually help me with mine.

Before we got started, I saw something in his eyes, the one thing I feared—hurt. I had hurt Jack. I wasn't strong enough to bring myself to say "I love you." Those three words would fix everything, and I was being a stupid girl who was too shy and too scared of letting down her guard to tell her boyfriend that she loved him. I didn't want to be scared, but I was.

I spent the next two hours hunched over Jack's notebook. It was the worst two hours of my life. Every time we accidentally touched, we'd pull away and say sorry under our breaths. We never looked at each other, and we barely spoke. I was scared of telling Jack I loved him, and it took me two of the worst hours of my life to figure it out. The reason was Leanne. Leanne had said she loved Jack way too early. It was only a month after they'd started dating, and everyone in school talked about it. Maybe somewhere in my subconscious I knew that. I didn't want to be a repeat of Leanne, which seemed to be a recurring problem in my relationship with Jack.

I would no longer be scared. At least, that's the lie that I told myself when I turned to him, touched his hand, and said the five words both of us had wanted to hear me say for the past two hours. I made sure to say them loud and clear: "I love you too, Jack."

His eyes lit up like I'd never seen them before. It was as if fireworks were going off in his head. He kissed me, and I finally felt those fireworks I'd always been longing for. It was the perfect romance novel kiss, at least before Tony broke it up and reminded us that it was a Saturday night at 8:00, which meant that it was family night at the restaurant.

Jack and I abandoned my English essay for the rest of the night. It was five pages, and all I needed to do was some light editing. Tony kicked us out when we started kissing again, but we ended up walking around town, just holding hands and talking under the stars and moon and occasional street light. I could have stayed with Jack and done that forever. In a weird way, I had to thank Bea, because if her party hadn't been canceled, then Jack wouldn't have left his voicemail in the first place.

At around midnight—because, yes, we could talk for hours—Jack walked me home and left me with a goodbye kiss. He invited me to his basketball game the next day. I promised I would come. When I went inside, my parents were too busy binge-watching their latest addiction to notice the time. I walked up to my room on a cloud and passed my little brother sprawled on his bed like a starfish, his arms and legs spread out. He had fallen asleep with his iPad still playing his favorite show full of fuzzy, colorful characters with names I could never remember.

I put the blanket over him and took the iPad. By the time I changed into pajamas and got into my own bed, I wasn't tired anymore, so I started to watch *Gossip Girl*. Slowly, my thoughts about Jack faded into the drama. I watched one episode after another. It was never my type of show before, but as much as I hated to admit it, it was *really* addicting.

Fast-forward ten and a half hours: I woke up, and my brother was sitting on the foot of my bed with the iPad playing that silly kids' show. I must've fallen asleep watching *Gossip Girl*, just like I always thought I would if I started to watch the show, but under different circumstances, of course. I always thought someone would make me watch it and I'd fall asleep out of boredom, not because I pulled a near all-nighter to binge-watch it. As I retraced my steps from the night before, I remembered kissing Jack and our walk under the stars and then . . . Jack's game. I forgot about Jack's game. I vaguely remembered him saying that it started at ten, which meant I was going to be late, really late.

When I got to the game, it was the end of the fourth quarter, and we were losing by a lot. I joined the crowd sitting on the home-team side of the bleachers, and I saw Jack standing along the sidelines, his hair damp from sweat. He was watching the game with his arms crossed, and he noticed me shuffling alongside the parents sitting in the crowd. He turned away without a nod or a wave, but I understood. He wasn't in the mood to say hi to me when his undefeated team was losing that badly. I was starting to think that coming to the game was a bad idea, and maybe I should have let myself sleep in, because the way he looked at me was as if the night before had never happened.

My thoughts started spiraling again. Maybe he realized that he never loved me at all and what we said to each other the day before was a mistake. I couldn't let myself be that negative. A person doesn't go from being in love with someone one day to not being able to look at them the next.

I looked around for a distraction and saw Grace sitting at the very back of the bleachers. She was alone and quietly writing in a notebook. I walked over to her and plopped myself down on the empty space next to her on the bench. She jumped back a little as if I'd startled her, and she slammed the little notebook shut. I didn't question her about it; I had better things to ask her about.

"Hey, I was just wondering . . . does Jack seem different this morning, like really angry or upset or something?" I asked.

"Well, how could you expect him not to? Everyone's been talking about it."

"He's upset that he told me he loved me and I told him I loved him back and now everyone's talking about it?"

Grace giggled, so that was clearly not the answer. "No, you know the sophomore ski trip?"

"Yeah," I hadn't been planning on going, but I was starting to reconsider.

"The resort they always use had a big fire. You remember Mark? His family has a private ski lodge upstate. They've offered to host everyone on the same dates at a discount."

Let me explain. Mark was Jack's backstabbing, cheating ex-best friend. Mark transferred to a different school earlier that year, in October. He'd claimed that his parents inherited a ski lodge in upstate New York. None of us believed him, though. We all thought that he was trying to make up some excuse to leave the school and leave the mess he had caused behind. I was surprised the lodge actually existed. Then I remembered Jack. He loved snowboarding and had been waiting for this trip all

70

year, and Mark was ruining it just like he ruined everything back in the fall. No wonder Jack was crushed.

"Oh," I said.

"That's it? There's going to be some serious drama going down, and that's only if he comes. Bella, you have to make him come!"

I didn't really know how to respond to that except for, "Okay."

Grace and I sat quietly for the next minute until the game ended. I never liked sports, so the loss wasn't as much of an upset for me as it was for everyone else. Once both teams shook hands, I rushed down to Jack. He looked at me and then looked away, as if we hadn't said we loved each other at all. Who knew Jack could be so emotional?

"Hey, Jack!"

"Bella, I'm not in the mood to talk right now."

"I heard about the whole thing with Mark."

"That's not it."

"That's gotta be some of it."

He stared at me. "Bella, our team just lost, and you ran down to the court to tell me about Mark? I can't think about anything else right now."

That last part was a lie, and we both knew it. Mark had ruined things for Jack in the past, and he'd most likely gotten into Jack's head and ruined his focus on the game, yet Jack wanted to place the blame on me, and I let him.

Seven

From Sunday on, all anyone could talk about was the sophomore ski trip. The girls' lunch conversations consisted of which store everyone was getting their jackets from and who they planned to hook up with, because the trip was notoriously known as the best hookup trip. I was not interested in where any of them were getting their jackets, and I already knew whom I was going to be hooking up with, so I was pretty quiet, except for when one of the girls would ask me for my opinion. I still couldn't get over how they actually valued what I thought.

Up until a few weeks ago, I had always thought that being quiet had helped me observe what was going on at school, but once I started hanging out with the girls, I realized that I was clueless when it came to so many things. It wasn't until I actually talked to them and hung out with them that I learned things. I was really starting to like the new person I was becoming.

Grace stayed unusually quiet during the girls' conversation too. I understood why she wouldn't want to chime in about the hookup part, because of her boyfriend back in Cleveland or Chicago, but for someone who had such a passion for fashion, her disinterest was strange. I wondered whether it was because Grace and Mark were friends when she first came to our school. Their parents had known each other for a long time, so maybe for Grace, going to Mark's family ski lodge was an extension of that familiarity. I didn't push her on why she was so quiet, though. I understood that we both had our reasons.

I felt someone tap my shoulder. I turned to see Jack.

"Hey, can we talk?" he asked. Jack had been off all week, ever since he heard about the whole Mark thing and his team lost the game. We'd barely hung out, but I was just giving him space.

"Yeah, sure," I said. As I got up from the table, I noticed Grace sitting rigid and still, her face flushed pink. One of the girls must have said something that made her feel uncomfortable. When I got back, I would have to ask her what it was.

Jack and I walked out of the cafeteria until we found a place that wasn't overpopulated with sophomores waiting to overhear pre–ski trip drama. After a few long, unbearable seconds of staring at each other, he looked down at his shoes and mumbled, "This was stupid; forget it."

"You wanted to talk, Jack, so talk."

"Right. So here's the thing: I don't want you to go on the ski trip."

"Is it because of Mark? Because you might not even see him there. You'll be outside, and he'll be —"

"I already told you it's not because of Mark!"

"Then what is it?"

He looked at me and then looked down at his shoes — his bright-yellow basketball shoes, which I'd always found ugly. He kept his eyes on them as he said in a quiet voice just loud enough for me to hear, "It's you and Mark."

Had I heard him right? I barely knew Mark, and he barely knew me. In a school where everyone knew everyone's name, I was positive Mark hadn't known mine. It wasn't like I would ever cheat on Jack with Mark. "I don't understand. I don't even like Mark. I barely know him."

"Bella, Leanne barely knew Mark until she did, and she didn't like Mark until they were making out. I'm sorry, but I don't want you to go on the trip. Mark gets what he wants, and he's going to want you."

I knew this conversation was hard on Jack, especially since he was usually reluctant to go back down memory lane. Still, I couldn't hide the disgust in my voice. "Why would he want *me*? I told you Jack—he barely knows me."

"I know how Mark works, okay? He was my best friend. He wants what I have, and I have you so . . . connect the dots. I don't want you to go on a trip where you're going to cheat on me. Even if you don't mean to, you will."

"Jack, I won't cheat on you. I don't want you to miss out on this. It'll be fun. You can teach me how to snowboard, and we can have hot chocolate and look at the mountains. Jack, I want you to come. I won't have fun without you."

"I bet you'll have fun with Mark," he said under his breath as if I couldn't hear him.

I didn't want to let myself cry, so I pretended that I didn't hear him and that he'd never said it in the first place. I told myself that this was the jerky side of Jack that didn't come out when he was with me, but that didn't mean it didn't exist. Leanne broke his heart, and he was still recovering. I wished it was easier for him to get over her, but I pushed the thought away, because *I* was Jack's girlfriend, not Leanne.

He stared at me for a moment to buy more time and said, "I can handle Mark. I just think that you shouldn't go. You don't know Mark like I do. I just don't trust him, okay?"

With an unexpected burst of confidence, I said, "You don't trust *me*, right? You think that I'm going to run off to Mark just like Leanne did and cheat on you. Is that it, Jack?" It felt good to get that off my chest. Sometimes I felt like I was Jack's Leanne replacement, but I didn't want to feel that way anymore. I didn't want to *be* that anymore.

Jack's face changed, and it was as if the jerky side of him took a leave of absence and the guy I fell in love with came back, at least for a little while.

"I'm sorry. I hear you," he said. Then he added, "It'll just be us? We can ignore him, right?" He sounded like he was trying to convince himself more than me.

"Right," I said with more confidence than I felt because, like I said, I barely knew Mark.

"I love you."

"Love you too."

We kissed, but it was quick — too quick — and then the universe was no longer ours. Some other sophomores were walking down the hallway in anticipation of the bell to ring that ended lunch. I used to be one of those kids who hated lunch. One, I found school lunch food to be disgusting and, two, my whole grade jammed into a small cafeteria was not how I wanted to spend my time. But that was before I talked to Jack. Before I knew it, Jack faded away into the jumble of students. I couldn't believe that at one point I had been thankful that I barely had any classes with him. Now, I thought it was a curse rather than a blessing.

At least it was Wednesday, and Wednesday meant writing club at the end of the day. I'd been sharing my work, but despite Jack's encouragement, I knew I wasn't that good at it. Jack was the true superstar. I felt that each time Jack got better, my writing kept getting worse. I still had fun hanging out with him, though, and we'd been keeping the tradition of going to Tony's afterward. For the rest of the day, all I looked forward to was hanging out with Jack.

I was so distracted with my thoughts about Jack that when I walked into English class, I didn't notice how Mr. Anderson was trying to stop me right as I walked through the door. Yes, Mr. Anderson and Ms. Anderson were married, and they taught English and history at my school. Mr. Anderson had liked me—not as much as Ms. Anderson did—but now they both seemed to hate me in a way I never knew teachers could.

Even before I sat down in my seat, Mr. Anderson said he'd like to speak with me outside. As soon as the class was settled, he joined me in the hallway. "I'd like to talk to you about your essay, Bella," he said.

"Did you like it, Mr. Anderson?"

"Here's the thing, Bella: I know you didn't write that essay. You couldn't have written that essay. Tell me: whom did you pay to write this?"

"I didn't pay anyone, and I definitely didn't cheat, Mr. Anderson."

"This is more than just cheating, Bella. Someone wrote this paper for you. You turned someone else's work in as your own. You could be suspended for that."

"I wrote that paper on my own."

"No one helped you?"

I couldn't lie, so I said, "Jack Walker helped me a little, but just with things like word choice and editing. He didn't write the paper for me, Mr. Anderson."

He sent me to the principal's office anyway. I knew that it was going to be bad. I knew that the consequences for plagiarism were going to be worse than receiving a disciplinary report or detention. The worst part was that I hadn't done anything wrong.

It wasn't my fault, and as much as I hated to admit it, it was Jack's.

Jack was the one who was making me into a different person, and even though I liked the different person I was becoming, it didn't seem to be helping me in any other part of my life. At the same time, I loved Jack too much, and I wasn't about to let every risk I'd taken and every single thing I'd done to make myself the person I'd become go to waste. I walked into the school office with these thoughts clouding my mind. I sat down in a chair and saw that Jack was already there, sitting in a chair across from mine.

"I'm sorry," Jack mouthed. He either was ashamed that he got me in trouble or didn't want the office lady to shush him. The whole joke about her eating Ms. Alperstein from the Jack and Luke Show had circled back to her, and she despised them. Whenever Jack was in the office, which was pretty often, she'd stare him down. Sometimes, Jack and I would joke that she secretly had a crush on him, but nothing having to do with him seemed funny at that moment.

"Bella and *Jack*, the principal's ready for you," the office lady said, stretching out the one syllable in Jack's name for a second too long. If it had been another day, we would've laughed together, but it was different now. From the corner of my eye, I saw Jack crack a small grin, but that was it, and as soon as it appeared, it disappeared.

We both walked into the principal's office, cautious not to touch each other. I needed Jack to give me some space, because we both knew he was the reason I was there. We sat down in the two chairs facing the principal's desk. His chair was turned away from us, until he attempted to do that thing that villains do in movies when they whip the chair around. But the chair squeaked, the turn was slow, and most of all, Jack and I both knew that the principal was already sitting there.

The look on the principal's face wasn't villainous or mean. He looked tired, and he typed some things into his computer and clicked his mouse. I thought I could predict the conversation we were about to have. He would say, "Bella, you're a good girl. Jack is a bad influence and always gets in trouble. You two shouldn't be spending so much time together. This relationship isn't good for you."

Instead, the principal started by asking us what we thought we did wrong. I could feel Jack smiling next to me, but other than that, I was lost. When we didn't answer, the principal got straight to the point and said, "This is plagiarism. You'll both be suspended from school for two days. Jack, you're already on disciplinary probation. I've warned you about this before, and you'll be off the basketball team for the rest of the year. This is going on both of your permanent records. I'll have to call your parents to pick you up."

We sat there, stunned. Then, Jack started arguing. The principal turned to me, as if Jack wasn't yelling at him, and said that if I didn't have anything else to say, I should wait for my parents to pick me up in the office outside.

Suspension for plagiarism on my permanent record. I couldn't wrap my mind around it. I never thought I would be suspended. Even though none of it was true, I had put my reputation on the line for Jack. I could no longer be trusted, which was a scary thought. I was now the type of girl who people believed would plagiarize. That was what I wanted, wasn't it? I never thought about the repercussions of it. I would have to explain to colleges the mess I had gotten myself into. I'd have to tell them that Jack had only helped me a little and explain that I was never a good English student. That didn't mean that they would believe me, though.

The second I walked out of the principal's office meant that I had surrendered. It meant that the image they had of me was true. What if I didn't want to be the bad girl anymore?

The principal's attention was taken by Jack, though, who was still yelling. I didn't know what else to say. The newfound confidence of mine had already gotten me into enough trouble, so I walked out of the office as the principal said something in a calming voice to shut Jack up.

When I got home, I lay on the couch and let my brain go to mush for hours as I watched some mind-numbing show on TLC. I also learned that TLC stands for "The Learning Channel"— who knew?

My mom had to come pick me up from school. It was strange to see her walking down the school's hallway, wearing a skirt and high heels, with the wind blowing cold outside. My parents had always let me do my own thing, especially since they realized I was nothing like them and would never be like them. They had always let me take care of school and grades on my own in the past. They believed that my grades were my own responsibility and didn't want to get involved. I had always thought that my mom had no interest in helping me with school, and my dad was always too busy with his job to care, so I was always left to my own resources.

But the thing was when I messed up, they got mad. They weren't the type of parents to ground me—instead, they'd bring up stories from when they were my age and tell me about how they never would have done what I did. They made me feel guilty and acted like whatever bad thing happened was all my fault, even though this time, my grades falling and getting suspended weren't entirely my fault—they were, at least in part, Jack's.

Driving home, my mom shook her head and said, "Isabella, I don't even know what to say."

"So don't say it," I said, staring out the window.

My mom dropped me off at home and left right away, probably to go to a girlfriend's house and talk about her issues with me as she sipped on a glass of wine.

As I watched TV, I thought about how my day was ruined, even though Wednesdays were usually my good days. That was the day I had writing and went to Tony's with Jack. It would have been the perfect day if Mr. Anderson hadn't decided to ruin it all. Jack, Jack, Jack. All that time spent at the writing club, at basketball games, at detention, at Tony's. All those late-night walks. All of those were distractions, really.

Even though my parents didn't do much to help me keep up my grades, they were still going to be mad if my grades were as bad as I thought they were. I was afraid to look at them. My grades had always been decent throughout high school. After spending forty-five minutes the summer before trying to calculate my GPA using three different grade calculator websites, I discovered that my cumulative GPA was 3.66, which was good. Now, I wasn't sure what my grades were, but they most definitely were not at a 3.66.

Even writing club had gotten different too. I didn't want to think about it when I was looking forward to seeing Jack there, but at the last session we'd been at, Jack had come in a bad mood. He wouldn't tell me why, but it didn't take a genius to figure out what had happened. Cynthia was there, the senior girl who'd led the first creative writing session I'd been to, and she gave us a "free writing" day, which meant that there was no prompt, so we could write about whatever we wanted. When we finished writing, Jack didn't encourage me to read but instead volunteered to be the first one to share.

He read fast and loud about his dad. I wasn't sure what he was trying to say, exactly, because Jack wrote in a way that used a lot of metaphors, but there was an anger in his voice that I couldn't shake, that seemed so different from the fantasy Jack I'd loved for years. Except, I needed Jack to be the fantasy I thought he was.

Cynthia gave Jack some generic positive feedback. He changed the subject and with the same anger in his voice asked why she thought she had the right to be in charge when she wasn't even there half of the time. He wanted to know why she was the one who was leading the group, if she liked writing at all. Cynthia shrugged and said that he could take it or leave it, but being the leader of a club looked good on college applications. It was then that I realized that I wasn't having fun anymore at the writing club.

On the sofa, bummed and stuck in my head about my problems — my parents, Jack, grades, getting suspended, writing club, not to mention Bea and having to confront her after running away from her at her house — I started to focus on the TV. I flipped through the channels until my eyes caught an episode of a show I'd heard about called *Riverdale*. All of a sudden, the seemingly innocent town of Riverdale I knew from the *Archie* comics took a dark turn. Betty went dark and tortured someone with maple syrup only to nearly drown them. Archie teamed up with an FBI agent to uncover the corrupt Lodge Industries, and Jughead joined a gang.

Somehow the absurdity of it all drew me in. I'd never been a huge fan of TV shows, but that was before I discovered their complexity. The characters were all more than they seemed at first glance. Archie wasn't just a football star, and Betty wasn't just a good girl. Although the show was realistic fiction, it seemed more like fantasy. The chances of the events in the show happening to a real high school student were slim, but maybe that was the appeal to it. The show was more of a fantasy than anything. It was relatable, all the while whisking the viewer off into a different world.

I let all of my other worries fly away. I couldn't get enough. As I was drawn in deeper, I realized there was so much universality to it. Everyone was a teenager at some point and could relate to the characters on-screen, even if they were played by actors who were ten years older. Once you were able to connect to the show and the stories, it didn't matter how crazy the plot lines became because at the core of it all there was some connection between the viewer and the character, even if it was small.

The problems in my life seemed dramatic enough. But I wondered whether seeing my life in a way that was like *Riverdale* would help me to escape my problems — or whether it would make the true issues beneath my problems more obvious. And, somehow, with all of these thoughts in my mind, I drifted off to sleep.

I slept until the doorbell rang and woke me up. I had a headache that came from some combination of watching too much TV and thinking about my ever-growing list of problems, so it took me a minute to process what was happening. It was ten at night, which meant that Henry was either sleeping or on his iPad. My parents were upstairs, most likely binge-watching their latest addiction. And there I was, still weary from sleep and letting the door go unanswered as it rang for a second time. It hit me that if I didn't answer the doorbell, my parents would come downstairs, and I wasn't in the mood to talk to them. I trudged to the front door, and opened it to see Jack standing on the stoop with his face twisted up in guilt. He was holding some kind of tool in his hand, but it was too dark to tell what it was. I knew that whatever he had on his mind was going to be one more thing that was supposed to be Jack's fault but would somehow end up being mine. With one look into Jack's blue eyes, I forgot about everything else as he said, "I need your help."

I didn't know how to react. I could tell I was going to be dragged into whatever trouble he was about to make. When my eyes adjusted to the dim lighting, I saw that Jack was holding a power drill. I wanted to help him, and I wanted him to get out of the dark place he'd landed in after what happened in the principal's office so we could be happy again, but did that mean I should do anything possible to accomplish that?

"Bella, I need your help," Jack said again with the same amount of guilt.

"I heard you the first time," I said. I really wasn't in the mood to talk more about what he planned to do with the power drill, but I also couldn't push him away, because that would push him further into his dark place.

"Sorry, I wasn't sure, so I just thought . . . "

I took a deep breath as I tried to figure out what to say next. "What do you need me to do?"

"I'm going to pop holes in the principal's car tires, and I need you to help me." He played with the drill. "I found this in my garage. You won't have to do anything but keep lookout."

I burst out laughing. I thought it was a joke. When I realized Jack wasn't laughing with me, I stopped. The look on his face remained serious. "Are you in or not?" he asked.

"No, Jack. You're insane. You can't vandalize the principal's car because you're mad that you're off the basketball team. I'm sorry that happened. I know you loved to play, and it was so much of who you were, but popping holes into anyone's car tires won't get you back on the team."

Jack's face remained dark, but it was as if what I said took the wind out of his body. He slumped and almost dropped the drill onto the ground. I was worried that one of my parents would come down the stairs and wonder what the heck Jack was doing standing at our door at ten at night with a power drill in his hand.

"Why are you doing this to me?" Jack asked.

"Why am I doing this to *you*?" I asked, lowering my voice to a whisper-shout. "I have a freaking headache, Jack. I'm exhausted, and you're asking me to pop tires on the principal's car with some shady power tool. Doesn't that sound even a little pathetic to you?"

His face softened, and he looked almost like the Jack I knew and loved. "I guess, maybe, a little but—"

"Go home, okay?"

He looked down at his hand and gripped the drill. "If you promise me that you'll help."

"Jack, we're not five. I'm not going to just pinky promise you so that everything will get better. Go home."

"Just come out with me. We'll go for a walk or something."

Was he serious? I had just asked him to leave two times. He wasn't listening to a thing I said, and I was stupid enough to think that was normal.

"No, Jack, I'm tired, so just stop bothering me, okay?"

"But Bella—"

"Good night, Jack," I said, and I closed the door before he could say anything else to make me keep it open for even a second longer. Even though I was starting to get to know a different side of him, he still did things to be that popular and obnoxious loudmouth I always knew he was.

But when I closed the door and left Jack in the cold, I felt bad. I didn't know where all of the confidence I just showed him came from. Two months ago, I would've agreed to anything he wanted me to do. I would've gone for a walk with him, and I most likely would have gone along with Jack's plan to pop the principal's car tires.

I went upstairs to my room, and for the first time, I thought about what would've happened if I hadn't walked into the writing club a few weeks ago. I could've survived the rest of high school without talking to Jack. I would still be friends with Jade, Makenzie, and Nicole. I wouldn't be worried about having bad grades, or getting detention, or being accused of cheating on an essay. I went to close my shades and promised myself that I would keep him out of my head.

I closed my shades, then opened them again, because I thought I had just imagined Jack standing there, half lit up by the garden lights. He was holding his notebook over his head, and I wondered for a second whether he'd totally lost his mind. I squinted to make out the words he'd scrawled in huge letters on the notebook paper: *Sorry*.

Then I remembered all of the things that had happened since I walked into the writing club a few Wednesdays ago. I started talking to Jack, I made new friends, I had a new best friend, and I got to live on the wild side for once and not just be the good girl everyone thought I was. I felt that the positive influences of Jack being in my life outnumbered the negatives, and as much as I wanted to stop myself, I couldn't, and I ran downstairs, opened the door, and watched Jack's eyes light up the night as soon as he saw me.

"I'm sorry, Bella."

"I saw," I said, nodding at his notebook.

"I didn't mean to come here and pick a fight with you."

It was hard to stay mad at Jack. I looked into his eyes that somehow always got to me, and the doubts I had about him vanished. I told him, "I forgive you."

Then he kissed me, and if my eyes had stayed open, I would've sworn that the stars glowed and danced around the moon. Most people would've said I was so in love—maybe even *too* in love—but no amount of love felt like too much to me. I couldn't stop. I loved the way he said "I love you," and I loved everything about him to the point where I couldn't believe I had fought with him or regretted talking to him.

When Jack and I got suspended from school, I also thought we wouldn't be able to go on the ski trip, which was scheduled for the next weekend. But we'd already paid for it, and the school said the decision was up to our parents, but either way, it was too late to get a refund.

All I did while suspended was sleep in and watch more TV—every teenager's dream. I watched all the seasons of both *Riverdale* and *Gossip Girl*. I couldn't get enough. By the time I went back to school on Monday, my parents had cooled off about the plagiarism fiasco. I'd told them Jack and I hadn't cheated, that it was all a big misunderstanding. I said that we had somehow gotten on the Andersons' bad side and Jack had really just helped me in editing the essay. I promised them I'd do better.

I got through the school week without getting into any more trouble, and on Friday, I managed to wake up extra early to pack for the ski trip, despite Jack's not-so-subtle hints that maybe I still shouldn't go. I didn't want to miss out because of him. I wasn't going to be that girl whose thoughts were dominated by Jack, and I wasn't going to let him dominate my actions too.

Once everything was packed and ready to go at 6:00 a.m., my dad drove me to school and shared stories of his own sophomore ski trip, which I only half listened to. My dad had been a big athlete, like Jack, and he used to ski all of the time, but my parents never bothered to teach me, and I never wanted to learn. When they realized I had no athletic talent whatsoever, they might've given up. I also thought it was strange that my dad was reliving his high school experiences, when they'd happened so long ago.

We pulled up in front of the school's auditorium, and I noticed the principal standing outside. I got out of the car, praying that he wouldn't notice me because I knew he hated me now too. I also really didn't want him to have any excuse to talk to my dad, who could make conversation with just about anyone. I got my mini-suitcase out of the trunk and left without even saying goodbye to my dad. I know it was stupid, but I really didn't want the principal to notice either one of us after he'd just suspended Jack and me. To my luck, the principal was too caught up with Luke blasting rap on his Bluetooth speakers to notice us. I turned and watched my dad drive away. There was a part of me that wished that my dad wouldn't have let me leave without saying goodbye, but my dad wasn't like that, or maybe he wasn't that kind of dad to me.

Inside the auditorium, the first one of my friends to arrive was Grace. She sat in the corner of the room, scribbling in that little notebook she'd had at the basketball game. I walked over to her, and she didn't notice me at first. I was curious to know what she was writing about, so I slid down next to her and tried to take a peek, but as soon as she noticed me, she slammed the notebook shut as fast as she could.

"What are you doing?" she asked, trying to hide the anger in her voice.

"Nothing." I didn't know what else to say, but I knew my answer sounded stupid. I stood up, and she sat in silence for a few moments, before I remembered that Jack hadn't arrived yet, so I really didn't have anyone else to sit with. "How are things going with your boyfriend back at home?" I asked to fill up the silence.

"Huh?" Grace said, staring off at the distance. "Oh yeah, fine."

We were quiet again. "Are you excited about rooming together?" I asked. Grace put her notebook into her backpack and smiled in the same way she had when we first became friends. "I came prepared," she said. "I brought my computer and made a list of movies on my Netflix account. If you've already watched them, that'll be even better, because then I could tell you about the costumes and actor gossip from the set."

"Oh, cool," I said. "I've never known that much about movies." I looked around us to see who else was there and noticed all of the kids I always thought were living in another realm of the high school experience than I was. I wondered whether we were all really that different. What gave Jack's friends some kind of unspoken authority to take up the room with Luke's music and their teenage boy jokes? They looked so happy and carefree as they threw basketballs at each other. How could they look so free when Jack, one of them, was making me crazy and so caught up in my thoughts?

I looked over at Grace, who was gazing off into the distance. What made Grace see me differently from the person I was before Jack? I glanced over to where my old friends were huddled in a corner, whispering about things I didn't know about anymore.

Was Nicole really that different from Heather? Was Makenzie really that different from Leanne? Then I looked over to the door as the rest of the girls walked in, led by Bea. They seemed to take up the whole room with their presence as they wheeled their mini-suitcases over to us. Everyone watched them as they walked toward us, and they loved the attention.

That was nothing compared to when Leanne walked in. The whole room seemed to be silent, except it wasn't for Leanne. Jack was right behind her, looking bored as ever. He didn't have any patience for anyone speculating any drama, so he shifted the shoulder strap of his duffel and pushed his way past Leanne and over to his friends without bothering to look at me. No hurt or anything that resembled it registered on Leanne's face as she walked over to Luke. Jack grabbed a basketball from one of his friends, but I didn't miss him looking at Leanne and Luke for what seemed to be a second too long. Before I could do anything, the principal announced that we were leaving.

When we got on the bus, I followed Jack to the very back seat and sat by the window. Even though our grade wasn't that big, it took an hour for all of the students to get on the bus, and then another half hour for the chaperones to take attendance. Finally, we set off for Mark's family's ski lodge in upstate New York.

I'd always preferred to sit by the window . . . that is, I did prefer it, until that bus ride. Jack and I were sitting next to each other, but we might as well have not been. We barely spoke, other than when I told him he was sitting on my jacket. I didn't know why Jack was acting so weird, and my window seat cornered me so that I was all alone and couldn't talk to anyone without touching Jack. Neither of us wanted that, and we both knew it without saying a word.

Jack ignored me but otherwise acted like himself. I remembered past school trips, when I sat closer to the front of the bus with my old friends and thought that everything fun seemed to be happening at the back. Now, Jack was that everything. He brought the perfect Spotify playlist to blast on Luke's Bluetooth speaker. He had all of the good stories. He had all of the funny jokes. I couldn't even bring myself to laugh with him, and I was stuck all alone in the corner. Eventually, I took out the earbuds I'd brought just in case I had nothing else to do and pressed shuffle on a playlist. I turned to Jack, but he didn't even glance at me; he was too invested in a conversation with Luke. I wasn't in the mood to listen to the Jack and Luke Show, so I fell asleep as the words from the song echoed in my head.

I dreamed of Jack. The dream came from a memory I had from a year and a half ago, when Jack was still in love with Leanne. I was walking home from school. Our town was so small that if I wanted to, I could pass by Leanne's house on the way to my house, and it made my walk only a minute or two longer. I chose to walk by Leanne's house that day, because I thought that maybe she would be standing outside in her yard. When she saw me walking by, I hoped it would be just her and me, like it used to be. Then she could feel like she could apologize to me, for ditching me for better friends, even though I knew I owed her an apology too.

When I got to Leanne's house, she actually was standing outside on her porch. But it was clear that she wasn't waiting for me, because she was with Jack. I stopped short because I didn't want either of them to notice me. Leanne was trying to tell Jack to leave in a voice that said she didn't really want him to go. "I can't talk right now; I have to do my homework," she said.

I wasn't surprised. After all, Leanne never wanted to do homework. That never seemed to matter, though, because she was crazy smart. For some reason, she wanted the least number of people possible to know how smart she really was. I always thought her smarts were one of the reasons why she and Makenzie got along so well.

"Leanne, I need to tell you something," Jack said. In my dream, I became Leanne, standing in the doorway. I saw Jack's eyes getting softer and softer. "I love you. I'm crazy about you," he said.

"Jack we're only fourteen," I said.

"Why does that have to matter? I've never felt this way about anyone else, and I don't think I ever will again. You're the only person who makes me feel this way. You're smart and clever and funny, and I love your laugh. You're daring, and you're caring—wait, that wasn't supposed to rhyme. Anyway, what I'm trying to say is that I'll never love anyone else the way I love you."

Then in my dream, I returned from being Leanne to just myself again, hiding behind a bush on the street, alone. Jack and Leanne kissed, and the worst part of it was that I believed what he said. He was more sincere with Leanne than he had ever been with me. The entire school had known how intense Jack's feelings were for Leanne, and people were jealous of them. Most of all, I was jealous of them. I believed Jack when he said he'd never love anyone the way he loved Leanne. They'd still be together today if she hadn't cheated on him, because they were the ones who were supposed to last through high school. It was supposed to be Leanne and Jack, not Bella and Jack. People had doubted us from the start, even though I loved Jack more than I had loved anyone else before. Did that also have to mean that Jack had to love me more than he'd ever loved anyone before? I wasn't sure.

"Bella, Bella, wake up. We're here."

I opened my eyes and saw Jack. All I could think about was how he would never look at me the way he looked at Leanne. It was more than just that—he'd never love me the way he loved Leanne.

I was willing to accept that. I don't know why, but I was. At least I wasn't the one who cheated on him with his best friend. At least I wasn't the one who broke his heart. As much as I tried to convince myself of Leanne's failings, if it was true that she ruined everything between them, then why did I feel that there was a part of him that still loved her? I knew I had been shaken up by a dream, but there were parts of it that seemed too real to be just a dream.

"Bella, we're going," Jack said, trying to wake me up again, this time from my daydream that was turning into a nightmare of thoughts.

Still groggy from sleep, I pushed myself off of the bus seat. As I walked down the aisle, I noticed Leanne's dark brown hair — with its new blond highlights that no one else could pull off — near the front of the bus, a few students ahead of us. The most important thing now was to get off the bus as quickly as possible *with* Jack. I usually tried not to pay that much attention to Leanne — I didn't want to be that crazy, paranoid girl, but as we stepped off the bus, I clasped Jack's hand.

As we walked toward the lodge, Jack stopped short, so I stopped too. He turned to me and said, "I'm sorry I was mad at you. I don't want to be mad at you, and I don't want things to be awkward, so can you just accept this apology?"

"Yes," I said, simply, even though I didn't feel like I had the power to fix everything by saying yes. I couldn't fix the fact that we fought, I couldn't fix the heart that Leanne broke, and I couldn't fix the fact that Jack loved her. When I got out of my head and started paying attention to Jack again, though, I realized he was already at the front door of the lodge, wondering what I was still doing standing where we were.

It seemed to him that my yes really could fix everything that easily, even if I didn't believe so. Maybe he just had a better attitude than I did, so I decided that I'd adjust my attitude, at least for the rest of the trip. I wanted Jack to be happy, and I couldn't be happy unless Jack was happy with me. Even though saying that to myself sounded a little pathetic, I couldn't live any other way.

The room assignments, the unpacking, and the overall beginning of the trip buzz passed by in a blur. Once we got our keys, Grace and I had to drag our suitcases up a really long flight of stairs since one of Jack's friends managed to break both elevators. I'd never been to a ski lodge before, but when we opened the door to see our room with two twin beds, it looked like any other hotel room, with a chair in the corner and a TV pushed up against the middle of a wall. We set our suitcases on the ground to unpack. I looked over to see that Grace had brought much more clothing than needed for a two-day trip. When she noticed my surprise, she put on a fashion show as she flipped through five different outfits. When she finally decided on the first one, a navy blue fleece over a beige base layer, we were already an hour late to the ski valet to rent our equipment.

When we got there, most kids were already done with the rental process. We weren't surprised to see that Bea, Mila, and Heather were just getting started. They must've spent just as long as Grace did when it came to picking their outfits. I turned my attention to the ski valets, who all wore uniform fleeces and looked like they were about twenty years old. They joked and laughed easily and were clearly used to being the center of attention. One of the valets walked over to Grace and asked her to come with him. I kept quiet as I waited for my turn. A guy who wore a winter hat and sunglasses walked over to me with a familiar strut full of confidence. I couldn't place him.

"Hey, Bella, heard about you and Jack," he said.

For a second, I was confused about how he already knew my name. He lowered his shades, and then it hit me — Mark was standing there right in front of me. His green eyes were cold and the exact opposite of Jack's warm blue ones.

"Hi, Mark," I said. Even though some part of me imagined Mark to be secluded in his room all day wallowing in guilt, regretting what he had done to Jack, the reality seemed a lot more practical. He was enjoying his new life backdropped by mountains and working as a ski valet after school—probably because he liked to check out girls who looked just like the girls at our school. He winked and flashed a smile, and I knew nothing had changed with him. Mark was still Mark, which meant Jack was going to be super pissed.

I didn't respond as Mark glanced down at his clipboard and asked, "What's your shoe size?" I knew I shouldn't be talking to him. What if Jack saw me?

"Is there someone else who could do this?" I asked, but with one look at Mark, I knew the answer was no.

"Everyone else is taken. They all chose their girls—"

"What?"

"All of the valets called dibs on the girls. Some guy, Vince, already chose you, so I had to pay him twenty bucks to get you," he said, as if it wouldn't bother me that he was talking about me like I was some object or prize to be won.

"Why would you pay someone?"

"Isn't it obvious? You're Leanne 2.0. Jack's new Leanne. I never saw the appeal, but I've gotta admit: I'm starting to see it now."

"What do you mean by 'the appeal'?" Even though I already knew how he would respond, there was a part of me that still wanted to hear him say it—because Jack had never said it—at least not in the way Mark would.

"You're kinda hot."

I blushed, and I realized I shouldn't have even asked him that question. I had to change the topic and remembered how I never answered his question. "I'm a seven," I said.

"You're not a seven," Mark said. "I'd give you at least a seven point five."

I rolled my eyes. "In shoes, I mean. I'm a seven."

"In case you didn't realize, that was me trying to hit on you."

"I did, and I have a boyfriend." As soon as I said it, it was fun to see jealousy spread across Mark's face. I knew we were playing some kind of game, but the fun of it all somehow made it okay.

"Oh, playing hard to get, huh?"

I realized that I shouldn't have pushed Mark, and I shouldn't encourage him to like me. Jack already liked me; in fact, he said he loved me. I had to get out of the stupid situation I had gotten myself into and the one that Mark had paid twenty bucks to get into.

"Can you please get me someone else? Because you're clearly not good at your job."

"Everyone else is taken, like I said, so you have me. And I am good at my job. If I wasn't, then I wouldn't tell you that ski boots and regular shoe sizes run differently, so like I said before, you're not a seven."

"I'm getting snowboard boots."

"You're a snowboarder. I did not see that coming."

"Yeah, Jack's teaching me."

"Classic Jack. He's a good snowboarder, but he's a bad teacher. I could teach you if you want."

"Can you please just get me boots and a board?" I asked, regretting the fact that I said "please." Why did I have to sound so polite?

"You sure you don't want me to teach you? I'm good; I swear. I even volunteer to teach little kids on the weekends sometimes."

I pictured Mark standing with a group of little kids in brightly colored jackets at the top of the bunny hill, and even after all of the other things Mark had said, my feelings about him softened a little. "He'd probably get mad," I said.

"I asked about you, not Jack. If you really want me to stop bothering you, just say you don't want me to teach you, and I won't—but tell me the truth."

I'd be lying if I said I didn't consider it for a few seconds, but in the end, Jack beat out Mark. "No, I don't want you teach me. Now can I get boots and a board before you waste any more of my time?"

"Okay, then, stand up and take off your shoes so I can measure your feet."

I did as I was told, but I could see disappointment in Mark's face. If I was loyal to Jack, then why did I feel like I just hurt Mark's feelings? Mark was supposed to be heartless, but was he not as bad as I, and everyone else, had made him out to be? He volunteered to teach little kids how to snowboard, and heartless jerks didn't do that. What if I was seeing the story all wrong this entire time? I'd heard the saying that there was more than one side to a story, and maybe Mark's version of what happened with Leanne didn't make him out to be the bad guy that Jack's version did. It was Jack's side of the story that I'd heard over and over again and the one that had created a particular version of Mark in my mind.

Mark let go of my foot and went behind a counter to get me boots and a board. I tried to convince myself that he was the victim of Jack's story, but I couldn't. I watched as some of the other valets called out Mark's name and nodded over to me without waving or meeting my eyes. Mark had the face of the boy who made funny—yet way too many—inappropriate jokes. He was the boy who picked on people so that he would feel better about himself. He was the boy who treated girls like they were objects, and he was the boy who hooked up with his best friend's girlfriend. This was the face of the boy who I'd heard again and again for so long was supposed to be the jerk. I'd heard it so many times, that I believed it myself. Mark shrugged in response to the valets and disappeared into the back room where the snow boots were stored.

If I was thinking about other sides of the story, I might as well think about Leanne's. I could see how she thought Mark was attractive—once she got past all of his bad qualities—and maybe he liked her too. Maybe Leanne had been mad at Jack, and maybe Mark just gave her the escape that she needed. I still couldn't understand, though, how Leanne could do what she did to someone who clearly loved her more than words could express.

I wanted to understand Leanne—and I was getting closer—but I just wasn't there yet. Jack was a good person who made a few mistakes, but none were like the ones Mark had made. Once I got to know Jack, I knew he was a good person, but I couldn't imagine Mark being a *genuinely* good person.

I was too busy in my thoughts to realize that Mark had returned with my boots and board in hand. He was waiting for me to answer a question that I hadn't heard him ask. "Do you want to hang out with me tonight?" Mark repeated his question.

"I thought you said you'd stop bothering me," I said. In truth, I was already feeling tired from waking up early, the bus ride, all the thinking I'd been doing, and this conversation with Mark. What I really wanted to do that night was curl up in my bed in the hotel room, watch movies with Grace, and listen to her side commentary on all of the set drama and actors' clothes.

"I said that I'd stop bothering you *for now*. It's later now, and I want to hang out with you. I'll take you anywhere in the lodge. I have total access. There's a bowling alley, or we can go to the kitchen, or—"

"Mark, I have a boyfriend."

"I know."

"So why do you keep asking me to go out with you?"

"Because I like you."

"You barely know me."

"You can learn a lot from someone in twenty minutes."

"What did you learn about me?"

"Well, let's see. Jack is your first boyfriend; I already knew that from before. But the way you're so possessive of him, it's like you use the fact that you have a boyfriend as an excuse to not take risks or have any fun. But it's more than that—you pretend you're not scared. You try to find excuses when you're uncomfortable in a situation or talking to a new person. You do things sometimes because other people are doing them or because someone wants you to do them, like Jack wanting you to snowboard, for example. I'm not sure whether that's because you've just been thrust into this whole new social situation where you have to hang out with Jack's crowd. You're afraid to lose this; even if you don't think so, you are. That's one of the reasons you're so scared to hang out with me. Oh, and you are a size seven."

I didn't know what to say. I wanted to protest, but that would just prove Mark right. I couldn't let him think that he was right about everything he said. I wasn't even sure whether he was wrong about anything he said. I'd always thought Mark was dumb, but clearly, I was wrong about that. I didn't know how he got so much from our short conversation, but one thing was certain: he listened. I remembered Grace telling me once that she'd learned he was a good listener from all the time they'd been forced to spend hanging out with their families. I didn't believe her then, but now, I could see what she meant. Mark could evaluate a person from listening to a sentence or two. Still, I couldn't let him know I was scared in any way. All I could think to say to him was, "Bye, Mark."

As I walked out with my boots and board in hand, I heard him say, "That means I was right about everything, right?" I didn't answer him, because maybe I wanted to prove him wrong, even though I knew somewhere inside of me that everything he said had been so on point that I hadn't even realized some of how I felt until he said it out loud.

Outside, Jack was sitting on a pile of snow and throwing handfuls of it into the sky. He looked bored out of his mind, and when he saw me, he got up and asked, "Where have you been?"

"I was getting boots and a board," I said, signaling to both items.

"Did you see *him*?" Jack asked.

"See who?"

"Mark. Grace told me she saw him working as a ski valet."

"No, I didn't see him," I lied, thinking that would be better for the both of us. I looked around. "Was Grace just here?"

"Yeah, just a second ago," Jack said. "Okay, so you want me to teach you how to snowboard, right?"

"I'm gonna suck."

"No, you won't. I'm a good teacher; I swear," Jack said, and I was spooked by how that last part sounded so familiar.

"No, Bella, you're supposed to go on toe side, not heel side. How many freaking times do I have to tell you that?"

Jack was getting frustrated. It had been two hours, and I still had no idea what I was doing. All I could think about was how maybe Mark was right about Jack being a bad teacher. I was thinking about Mark more than I wanted to, and I couldn't focus on what Jack was trying to teach me, so maybe it was my fault that I couldn't learn, not Jack's. I wasn't thinking straight. Was it really the thought of *Mark* that made my brain go to mush? If anyone was supposed to make my brain go to mush, that person was supposed to be Jack.

"I think we should stop," I said.

"Yeah, I think so too. Maybe we can try again tomorrow," Jack said, but I could tell by the tone of his voice that he didn't really mean that last part. I was a lost cause.

"Do you want to do something later?"

"What were you thinking?" I asked, even though by then I was exhausted and didn't have any intention of saying yes.

"Some of us are going to the hot tub," he said, smiling.

"I thought we weren't allowed." If I remembered anything from the speech that the lead chaperone had given us before he gave us our room keys, it was that we weren't allowed to go to the hot tub.

"We're not, but no one's gonna catch us," Jack said.

"I didn't bring a bathing suit," I said, trying to come up with some viable excuse. I thought again about curling up in bed and watching movies with Grace as she lent me her funny side commentary.

"It's fine. I bet you can borrow one from your friends," Jack said. He was obviously not getting the message.

"I'm not sure I want to go." I had to come right out and say it. If I didn't, I could tell he was going to drag me into it, eventually.

"It'll be fun," he said as he tried to come up with another reason for me to go. "Grace is going." So much for the night I had been planning.

"When did she tell you that?" I said. "She didn't say anything to me."

"Just earlier. Everyone'll be there."

"I'll think about it," I said.

After standing there for a minute, watching the sun sink lower toward the mountains and not knowing what else to do with ourselves, Jack asked, "Do you wanna head in for dinner?"

"Yeah," I said, because there was nothing else to say to him. Throughout the whole trip, I hadn't known what to say to him. First, he'd ignored me, and now it wasn't like I could tell him that there was a chance I might have a small crush on his ex-best friend, who'd caused his ex-girlfriend to cheat on him. That would be crazy, especially since Jack said that exact thing would happen. Anyway, a small crush was nothing compared to love, and Jack said he loved me. Despite that, I couldn't shake the nagging feeling that Jack wouldn't ever love me like he'd loved Leanne.

I was too caught up in my thoughts to realize that Jack was holding out his hand and waiting for me to take it. I must have waited too long, because he let his hand fall to his side as he turned away and headed toward the lodge.

Nine

I looked at myself in the mirror. I was wearing Grace's spare baby-blue bikini. I always hated wearing bathing suits because of how revealing they were and how uncomfortable they made me feel. Who wanted to see some of my butt cheeks? I didn't even want to see them. One-pieces were bad enough, but all Grace had was a bikini, and it seemed the other girls had brought only bikinis too. The bikini Grace gave me was meant to show off the curves that I didn't have, which made me feel even more uncomfortable.

"You ready?" Grace poked her head into the bathroom. She must have mistaken the look I was giving myself in the mirror as admiring, because she added, "What did I say? It's perfect on you, right?"

I kept staring into the mirror, thinking about every other thing about my body I didn't want people to see. There was my outie belly button, which I'd always been embarrassed about. There were my too-skinny hips that gave me no figure. I turned away from the mirror and went back into our room, watching Grace confidently walk around in her navy-blue bikini, as if it were what she wore every day. I didn't think I'd ever have that much confidence about anything. I tried to wrap my arms around myself so my torso would be covered, and yet I also felt the part of myself that wanted to escape the weak shield my arms were trying to make.

Grace grabbed an oversized hoodie and put it over her bikini. "You want to wear yours too?" She asked. Without waiting for an answer, she walked right to the room door and opened it. Before I could say anything, I grabbed a hoodie from my suitcase and zipped it up. I followed her to the hallway, where she played look-out, overdramatizing every little movement, to the point where I laughed out loud and *almost* forgot that I didn't want to go to the hot tub in the first place. Grace scampered down the hall like a bank robber. She turned to me to make sure I was coming, so I closed the door behind me. As soon as the door slammed shut, I realized I didn't have our room key. I looked over at Grace, who somehow read my mind as she waved the room key over her head. Relief washed over me as I walked toward her, but then she motioned for me to stop. She then mouthed a bunch of things and used a lot of extravagant hand motions until I understood that she wanted me follow her lead. I scampered down the hall just as she had done, and when I reached her, we broke into laughter. That made me think that maybe the hot tub thing wouldn't be as bad as I thought it would, at least not with Grace by my side.

Our room was on the second floor, so we needed to cross an indoor terrace-like thing that overlooked the lobby and take a stairwell down. We didn't see anyone—no chaperones or kids who would tell on us. A thought crept up on me that I used to be one of those kids, but as soon as it came, I was able to push it away. Grace led the way, and when we walked into the hot tub area, it was clear that the party was already in full swing.

The lights were dim, but the room was packed. Luke had brought his Bluetooth speakers and was blaring loud rap music.

It was so loud that I wondered why no one had caught us yet, but looking around, I saw that no one else seemed to be worried, and so I decided I wouldn't be either. The room was full of steam, and the hot tub was crowded. Luke was sitting in the water talking up a storm. I saw how one of his eager listeners was Jack, who hadn't yet noticed me come in. Then the sequins on Bea's bathing suit caught my eyes. She was sitting on a beach chair, with each of the other girls on either side. Bea had ignored me earlier when we were waiting to get on the bus, and now she kept her face turned away from Grace and me. I was pretty sure she was glaring at me when we walked in. Did my running out of her house a few weeks before really make her that angry?

Grace pulled off her oversized hoodie to reveal her bikini. Through the dim lighting, I saw how she was also perfectly tanned, which I thought was kind of odd for early March. She walked in front of where the boys were sitting in the hot tub. Some of them, led by Luke, whooped and hooted at her. She ignored them as she slipped into the hot tub, letting the warm water envelope her. I wanted to do that. I wished I could do that, but I couldn't. I wasn't as comfortable as Grace was with herself. I wanted to feel good in a bathing suit, but all I felt was awkward and the need to keep my hoodie on. I could feel the boys' expecting eyes turn to me, especially Luke's, which creeped me out, but what I didn't notice before was that there was a girl under his arm — Leanne.

I realized that Jack was sitting next to Leanne, who was nestled beneath Luke's arm. At first, I thought I was being paranoid and making up what I was seeing, but through the steam and the commotion and the crowd of people in the hot tub, Jack and Leanne were talking quietly and smiling together, as if nothing else was happening. I needed to get out of the room and get Jack out of that hot tub, and somehow he still hadn't noticed me standing there.

I walked over to where he was sitting and asked, "Jack, can I talk to you?"

For the first time that night, Jack looked over at me, and his eyes lit up, but they looked different. They could've been brighter for me. I'd seen them turn brighter for me before. Leanne was sitting only inches away from Jack, and she didn't say hi or meet my eyes. She simply turned away to listen to something that Luke had to say.

"Yeah, come in," Jack said, motioning to the hot tub that I definitely wasn't going into.

"No, I meant outside. I want to talk to you privately," I said.

All of his friends *oohed* as if he were in trouble, but what they didn't understand was that if I didn't get him out of that hot tub, I'd be the one in trouble.

Luckily, Jack didn't argue as he pushed himself out of the hot tub. "Yeah, sure."

I'd seen Jack shirtless before, but I was struck by the sight of him: water droplets glided down his chest and made him shiny. The features of his face seemed to emerge from the darkness and dim lighting. He looked different and much more handsome than earlier in the day when he was frustrated about teaching me how to snowboard. I felt like I was falling in love with him all over again. He shook his head to dry his hair, and that just made me love him more. Was my attraction to him only physical? I didn't want that. I didn't want to be in love like that. I remembered a time back when Leanne and I were best friends, and I told her that when I was in love with someone, it wouldn't matter how they looked. It only mattered what they were like on the inside—so why was I more in love with Jack's appearance, as if his personality didn't exist? But with him standing before me dripping wet, I knew something had changed. I just couldn't quite place it. Jack grabbed a towel, and as he wrapped it around his waist, it hit me that I was jealous. I was jealous of Leanne.

"So what did you want to talk about?"

We walked away from the hot tub and toward the window, where we could see the night and stars. I had been so preoccupied with trying to get Jack away from Leanne that I hadn't actually come up with an excuse to keep him out of the hot tub. He looked at me intently as he waited for me to talk. I had to think of something to say. I wanted to make him jealous, the same way that my seeing him talk to Leanne in the hot tub made me jealous. "I need to be honest with you. I did see Mark earlier, when I was getting my boots and board."

"What?" Jack asked.

It made me feel good to see Jack care, so I continued. "And you were right. He did hit on me. He said that you were a bad teacher and offered to teach me how to snowboard himself. But I told him to leave me alone, and he did, eventually." I noticed myself rambling, but it was only because I needed to get Jack away from Leanne. All I wanted was his undivided attention, but was it worth telling him everything? "I just thought you should know."

I thought Jack was going to say that he would kill him—and a part of me wished he had—but he didn't. Instead, Jack stood still for a minute as he took in the news. Then his face softened. I remembered seeing the way he and Leanne talked earlier in the hot tub, and I wondered whether his feelings were less hurt because talking with her made his heart less broken. Or maybe it was that he actually cared less about me because his true love was pulling him toward her again. I couldn't decide which it was, but I wished that he would freak out the way he had when we were planning on going on this trip and that he would say something like how he wouldn't leave my side for the rest of the trip. After a long pause, he said, "Okay. I need to go have a talk with Mark.

You shouldn't be pulled into whatever crap we have going on between us."

I was surprised to see this side of Jack. Since when did he ever take the high road out of any drama? That was nothing compared to my surprise about the fact that he would willingly talk to Mark. I had to beg Jack to come on a trip where there was only a chance that he might see Mark. I didn't know how to respond, so I just said, "So we're good, then?"

"Yeah, we're good," Jack said.

I said I was glad to clear the air—or the air that I had created to get his attention—but did that really make a difference?

He pulled me in for a hug, letting the warmth of his skin engulf me until I let myself forget about all of the internal Jack drama I had created for myself. There was my small crush on Mark that I definitely wasn't going to tell him about, not that it mattered, because I was going to shrink it until it disappeared from my conscience. Then there was the whole Leanne jealousy thing, but I was convinced that it was all paranoia and I was making it all up. Things were finally going to be good between Jack and me again—great, even—and to solidify our future, I said in a soft voice, "I love you."

"I love you too, D," he whispered.

I froze in his arms as all of the warmth from his body evaporated into the air and went somewhere far away. I wanted to be happy that I wasn't paranoid and had been right all along, but I couldn't be. Even if Jack had noticed what he said and apologized that he slipped up, it wouldn't have mattered. He still loved Leanne.

I remembered it like it was yesterday. Last year, Jack and Leanne were sitting behind me in Spanish class, whispering and laughing, being annoyingly couple-like. We had an assignment to write about ourselves in Spanish, not that anyone followed that last part of the instructions. Jack and Leanne were constantly sneaking glances at each other's papers. Leanne decided to write her full name, middle name included, even though she had always been embarrassed about it. Jack read it, but when Leanne noticed Jack staring, she covered her name with her hand.

"Don't laugh! I don't like my middle name," Leanne told him.

Jack didn't laugh but said, "So you do have flaws after all? I guess that makes you human. And if you're human, that just means I'm going to end up falling harder for you, Leanne D—"

"Don't say it," she said, smiling.

"Fine, I won't say it now, but don't be surprised if I start calling you 'D' when I can't use words to describe how much I love you. Hey, but for now, maybe I can write a poem about it—and you'd never guess what I'm going to call it."

"What?" she asked, playing along.

"Delphine."

I remembered sitting in the classroom, not being able to focus with all of their whispering and laughing. Only now, still in Jack's hug, did I realize that I felt the same way—jealous—and nothing had changed. I shook myself out of Jack's arms, outside of his security, and all of the thoughts that had haunted me came back. I took one look into Jack's eyes, and I saw how they were confused. He didn't even realize what he said. If I told him, he would just apologize and tell me it wasn't true, that I'd misheard. I didn't need to hear him lie, so I ran out of the room.

Grace must have been the only other person in the room who understood how I'd been waiting for a chance to get out from the second we'd walked in. As I ran, I could hear Jack's pleas for me to come back, but Grace told Jack that he should just leave me alone, so she must have gotten how much I didn't want to be there. I kept running, not really sure where I was going, because Grace had held onto our room key.

When I got to the second floor, I stopped to analyze my surroundings. To get back to my room, I had to cross the indoor terrace that overlooked the lobby. I didn't know what I would do once I got there, other than stand in front of the door in my hoodie and bikini and just wait to get caught by a chaperone patrolling the hall. Still, I prayed that no one was sitting in the lobby ready to yell at a student. When I dared to peek, there was only one person sitting on the couch, watching a sports game. I forgot to add Mark to the list of people I didn't need to see in the lobby. I couldn't face him after what had just happened with Jack, because I'd just end up spilling what happened, and he'd lure me into cheating with him or something, just like Jack had said. But then again, why was I listening to anything that came out of Jack's mouth anymore?

I looked back at Mark one more time and convinced myself that I could walk across the terrace without him noticing. I hoped the volume on the TV was loud enough or that he was just too engrossed in the game to notice anything else, but as I moved, Mark looked up at me, amused.

I couldn't think of anything to do but freeze. Then I gave him a sheepish wave and said, "Hey, Mark."

Saying his name felt much better than it should have. Even though he was just like any other person—not my boyfriend and not Jack—it was like I didn't need him to be my boyfriend to feel that we had some connection, some secret understanding.

"How was the hot tub?" Mark whisper-shouted up at me.

"How did you know?" I whisper-shouted back.

Mark dug into his pants pocket and waved a set of keys in the air.

"Oh," I nodded.

In a normal voice, Mark said, "I'm guessing that bowling doesn't sound too bad right about now."

I put up a finger to my lips to signal him to be quiet. "I could get in trouble," I whisper-shouted.

"You'll be fine; teachers love me," he said at normal volume. Then he couldn't help laughing at his own joke; "Okay, no, they don't, but my parents own this place. How much trouble could you get in?"

"Mark, I really think I should go."

"What, you're afraid your precious Jack is going to find out?" Mark said, and for some reason, he'd known exactly what to say. I needed a night to not think about Jack, to not worry about Jack, and to not give myself the chance to play "I love you, D" over and over again in my head.

I knew Mark could be that distraction, even though I told myself that he was the last person I'd want to hang out with, so I whisper-shouted to him, "No, I'm not afraid," because for once, I really didn't feel afraid.

"Then why don't you come down here so we can continue this conversation?" Mark asked, turning back to the TV without waiting for my answer, as though he already knew I would say yes.

When I got downstairs, Mark motioned for me to sit on the couch seat next to him. Even though we were sitting in the middle of the open lobby past curfew, I felt safe being near him. He was an outsider from all the drama that was brewing in the hot tub area, and he was an insider to the ski lodge, so I didn't think we could get in too much trouble if a chaperone saw us talking together. I could lie and say that Mark and I were family friends, just like he and Grace were.

I sat down and expected Mark to ask me something about myself or about what happened that evening, but instead he looked at my legs and asked, "Why aren't you wearing pants?"

"Remember the hot tub?" I said, pulling down my hoodie.

"Right. Enlighten me."

"Maybe we can talk about something else," I said, not really in the mood to go into details.

"Just tell me, already," he said.

I looked into his eyes as I debated what to do. His green eyes were a stark contrast to Jack's blue ones. Mark's eyes challenged me, dared me, and even scared me a little—not that I would tell him that—while Jack's eyes were comfortable and safe. I should say, they *were* comfortable and safe, right up until he called me "D." I had assumed that Jack's character was predictable in contrast to Mark's, but maybe I had been wrong all along, which seemed to be a pattern with me when it came to Jack. Maybe Mark was really the predictable one in his challenging and daring nature. A part of me wanted to believe that, while another part thought I was just telling myself what I wanted to hear. I looked again into Mark's green eyes and told him everything, the entire story.

I told him all of it, from how Jack and I started talking to how he said he loved me. I pretended that I didn't see the spark of jealousy in Mark's eyes. I went on to tell him about how everything seemed to have been going downhill since then, about how Jack and I almost immediately started fighting and got suspended, about how even though Jack hadn't told anyone yet, he'd gotten kicked off the basketball team for the rest of the season. I described how Jack had come to my house and wanted my help to vandalize the principal's car. Then I said how I thought most of Jack's problems had something to do with Mark himself. In response, Mark just laughed, but I could tell some other sort of emotion was bubbling inside of him. Then I decided to just shift the topic to my friendship with Grace and the stupid girl drama I had with Bea. He was a surprisingly good listener for someone whom I believed was so arrogant, but then again, I had thought that Jack was arrogant too.

Eventually, I got tired of talking and found that I had pretty much exposed myself to Mark without taking off the big hoodie I was still wearing. As the room became quiet, I thought that maybe it was a good time for me to go, but to him, it meant that we were just getting started.

"Okay, Bella, now it's my turn," Mark said.

"I'm kind of tired," I said, which was true, even though I was using it as an excuse to not hear Mark's thoughts.

"C'mon, I thought we were having fun," Mark said, in a way that made me start to think that what we were doing was bad. I wondered whether us talking on the couch, and me telling him everything I just did, was just as bad as us messing around. I told myself that I wasn't cheating on Jack. I would never do that, even though things weren't great between us at the time. I told myself to just shove that small crush I had on Mark down a little further, because I wasn't going to cheat on Jack.

"I think I should go," I said again without moving. I knew willing myself to get up wasn't going to be easy.

"What, you don't want to hear about me? Are you really that self-centered?"

"I'm not self-centered," I said, but even I could hear the shakiness in my voice. I'd be lying if I said I'd been anything along the lines of "selfless" those past few months.

"If you're going to go, because you're so sure of who I am, then why don't you enlighten me?" Mark asked.

"I never said that." I didn't like the way he was twisting my words to benefit himself and hurt me.

"Then are you afraid? Are you afraid to get to know the real me? Are you afraid that I'm really not the 'bad guy', and if you stay to talk to me for one more minute, you'll see that?"

How did he do that? How did he manage to tell me exactly what I was thinking, before I even realized it myself? I thought about how maybe Mark wasn't really the "bad guy" earlier that day, but mainly, I didn't want to be afraid of things anymore. I was done being afraid. I needed to become a different person from the cowardly girl I'd seen in the mirror earlier that night, with her arms wrapped around her torso. I needed to prove that to myself, and I needed to prove it to Mark.

"I'm not afraid," I said, almost believing myself.

"Then give me your breakdown of me in twenty seconds."

He wanted to hear what I had to say about him in twenty seconds? How did he even come up with that number?

"I'm waiting," he said.

I wasn't going to hold back. "You're the obnoxious douchebag kid who no one would hang out with if you didn't strong-arm situations to make people like you. You twist up people's words to make them seem like they're saying things they're not actually saying. You can read people to the point where it's kinda creepy, but not creepy enough to turn someone away. You're smarter than you want people to know with the whole reading people thing. And your eyes, they're like really green and dark, but now that I'm looking at them maybe they're not so—"

I didn't realize I was rambling until it was too late. Jack had warned me not to hang out with Mark, but it was too late. I didn't realize that I had given Mark the chance to do what he wanted until it was too late. I felt his lips on mine, and by the time I pushed him away, it was already too late. The kiss had happened. As I got up, Mark looked at me with pleading eyes and tried to grasp my hand to get me to stay, as if he hadn't messed up what could have led to some strange friendship. I ran out of the lobby and up the stairs. I couldn't turn back time and change the fact that Mark had kissed me, because it was too late.

Ten

ours later, I still couldn't fall asleep. There was a sinking feeling in my stomach that wasn't allowing me to relax enough to sleep. I had to come up with a plan. A plan for Jack to never find out what happened. Then maybe Mark would forget the kiss happened, and I could eventually forget it too. But after hours of lying in bed and coming up with nothing, I was starting to believe that it wasn't possible. I looked over at Grace, who was sleeping peacefully, just as she had been when I ran into the room after Mark kissed me. I had prayed that she was asleep, and when I got to our room, I saw how she had left the room door open a crack by closing the hinged metal lock into the doorframe. Now I wished she was awake so I had another person in the room I could talk to.

I needed something to take my mind off of the whole Jack-Mark-Leanne dilemma. Grace's notebook was sitting on her nightstand. It would be so easy for me to reach over and flip the notebook open to a random page and read something—one of her problems, even—to take my mind off my issues. The more I thought about the idea, the more curious I became. The way she was always writing in the notebook and slamming it shut was suspicious. What could she possibly be hiding every time she saw me coming? I doubted her problems were bigger than mine, but still, I couldn't open her notebook and invade her privacy. I imagined what would happen if I wrote all of my problems down in a physical notebook that anyone could look at. Jack would probably break up with me, and I wouldn't blame him, because I'd do the same. But that would happen only if Jack found out about the kiss between Mark and me, and he wouldn't—at least not if I could help it. I'd always lacked good planning skills, and I still didn't know what I was going to do. I decided that lying in bed wasn't going to help and that getting up and walking around would be better than being alone in the emptiness of my dark hotel room.

I looked over at the digital clock on the nightstand: 5:32 a.m. Even though we were told that we weren't allowed out of our rooms until at least 7:00, I decided to get up and walk around. I put on my hoodie, the same one I'd worn over my swimsuit just hours earlier, and stepped out cautiously, making sure that I wouldn't wake up Grace as I shut the door behind me.

The hallway was lit by fluorescent lights. I felt relieved to be there, instead of being trapped in my own head in the darkness of the room. At the end of the hall was a small window that glowed softly with the first blue signs of morning. I still didn't know where I was going to go, so I stood with my back against the door and slid down against it until I was sitting on the floor. I closed my eyes and took a deep breath. I hoped that some genius thought would come to me—not that I'd ever been called a genius, which I should have taken as an indication that there wouldn't be any genius thoughts coming to me anytime soon. I opened my eyes to see a shadowy figure approaching from the other end of the hall. I wasn't even afraid at this point of getting caught by a chaperone. It was early enough in the morning that I could say I had just woken up. As the figure approached, I could tell it was a boy, a student maybe, but I couldn't be sure. There wasn't any good reason anyone would be outside of their room at this hour, and yet something made me stay out in the hallway.

"Yo, Leanne 2.0!" Mark said, way too loud. "What are you doing out here?"

Why did I stay and wait to see who was coming? I should have known it was Mark, the only person my age who wouldn't be in trouble for roaming the halls at a strange hour. I couldn't talk to him anymore, especially since he made me feel so powerless and confused. And if I kept talking to him, he wouldn't be the only one calling me Leanne 2.0. If I kept talking to him, Jack would flip out, and I couldn't let that happen.

"Yo, Leanne 2.0! I'm talkin' to you," Mark said, approaching me from down the hall. He looked like he'd just gotten up. His hair was sticking up in the back, and he was wearing sweatpants.

I put my finger again to my lips. "Shh!" I said.

"Right," he said, and when he got to where I was sitting, he sat down beside me, too close, as though we were already co-conspirators in some plot he'd hatched. He yawned, then asked, "Can't sleep, Leanne 2.0?"

"Can you please not call me that?" As I heard my plea, I realized how weak it made me sound. Why did I have to say "please"? It made me sound like some polite girl who cared too much about manners.

"I'm just trying something new." Mark shrugged with a stupid smile plastered onto his face.

"I don't want to talk to you," I said, and once again I regretted how I sounded. Why couldn't I think of anything snappier, or something that could hit him hard in the gut, or even the heart?

116

Then with a different tone of voice, he said, "Then just listen to me. I promise you don't have to talk if you don't want to." Why was he pretending like he was Mr. Nice Guy all of a sudden? The change in his voice made me suspicious, and I didn't need him to be Mr. Nice Guy. In fact, I didn't need him at all.

"Why should I listen to you?"

"Because Jack's not the guy for you," Mark said, staring at me with cold, dead eyes. A chill ran down my spine, and the change in his voice made me suspicious. Why would I believe him? He read my expression and continued, "Jack's too hung up on Leanne. He's still in love with her, and you're too blind to see it."

"So your solution was to kiss me?"

"No, it was—"

I cut him off because I didn't care what he was going to say, "Then why'd you kiss her? Was it because you were jealous of your best friend for having a stable relationship when you're not capable of ever having one? Is that it? Because, honestly, Mark, I'm having trouble understanding what your logic is with any-thing you do. What kind of joy do you get out of ruining your best friend's relationships?"

What I said must have stung, because for a moment, Mark just sat there staring at me, without saying anything.

"What kind of story did you hear about Leanne and me?" he asked. "That has nothing to do with why I'm into you. Calling you Leanne 2.0 was just a joke, 'cause you're a repeat for Jack."

"What do you mean, 'what kind of story did you hear?'"

He stopped to think about what he was going to say and avoided eye contact by staring at the closed door of the room where Grace was sleeping. "Just forget it; it's nothing. I should go. It was a stupid idea to come here in the first place."

"Then why did you come? How did you know I'd be here?" I asked, confused.

"Like I said; it's nothing," he said, getting up. Then, crouching with his arms on his knees, he brought his face close to my ear and lowered his voice to a whisper. "I don't want to see you getting hurt too," he said, and before I could ask him any more questions about the most confusing thing he'd said, he got up and walked away.

Why was I going to get hurt? What secret was he hiding? Was it even his secret, or was he covering for someone else? And the most confusing question was who *else* was he talking about when he said that he didn't want to see me getting hurt *too*?

I couldn't shake the feeling that I was being drawn into some kind of elaborate web. I needed to think some more about everything that was happening before I talked to anyone, so when I walked back into the room and saw that Grace was still asleep, I was relieved. As I slipped back under the covers, though, I noticed that her notebook had shifted a little since the last time I saw it. It could have just been my imagination, though, because it was dark, and I was definitely exhausted. Why would Grace hide the fact that she was awake anyway? I could just imagine her getting a kick out of overanalyzing the conversation that had just happened between Mark and me, hiding on the other side of the door and scribbling it all down. With these strange thoughts in my head, I fell asleep.

"Wake up, wake up, wake up!" A pillow whacked my face.

For a second, I forgot where I was. I thought I was at home and that Henry was waking me up with one of his usual annoying methods. Just for a second I forgot that the night before had happened. I forgot that I was an emotional roller coaster with my feelings about Jack. I forgot what he'd called me, and I forgot my conversation with Mark. I forgot how he kissed me,

I forgot lying sleepless in my bed for hours, I forgot my second conversation with Mark, and I forgot the last thing that he said to me that left me wondering about what he meant. Then it all came rushing back to me like a flood. I'd never broken anyone's heart before. Was it supposed to feel like you were breaking your own too?

I opened my eyes to see Grace, crouched over me with a pillow in her hands. When she saw my face, she asked, "Bella, you okay?"

"Yeah, yeah," I said, because I didn't know how to say that I was feeling the exact opposite of okay after getting something like two hours of sleep.

"C'mon, get up, get up, we've gotta go to breakfast," she said with so much excitement in her voice that I almost didn't believe it. What kind of teenager was that excited for breakfast? The room smelled like coffee. Had she made some? I made a sort of grunting noise and turned over, hoping she would understand that I wasn't in the mood to talk or to do anything, really—and she did. She just laughed and didn't leave me alone. "What happened last night?" she asked, sitting on the bed.

I did the first thing that came to mind—deny. "Nothing," I said.

"Bella, I'm not an idiot. I know you're hiding something. Just tell me."

I flopped over to look at her. "You can't tell anyone." I felt like if she did, my life would be ruined.

"I won't; I promise."

"Okay . . . " I looked at her face and hoped that she wouldn't judge me. "Mark kissed me."

I waited, and Grace reacted in some sort of delayed way, as if it took a minute for what I'd just said to sink in. Then her eyes widened a bit, and she let out some kind of gasp as if she were shocked—but it was a strange reaction and one I hadn't exactly expected. The silence was killing me, though. I wanted to know where I stood with her. She'd been close friends with Mark before she became friends with me, so I wanted to hear what she had to say.

"Tell me what happened," she said. Her face remained expressionless and showed no indication as to how she really felt. For a second, I looked at Grace and wondered whether she would stay on my side. Was she asking me to tell her what happened because she wanted to give me advice? Or was she asking me so she could spread rumors about what happened and overexaggerate every detail? Then I felt bad for even thinking that and for doubting Grace, because, of course, I knew her reasoning was the former. Still, sometimes good people can do bad things, even those whom you trust the most. I needed to make sure she was truly my friend who would stand by me no matter what and not just a "friend" who would bolt and betray me when everything wasn't perfect. I wasn't going to find out until I told her the whole story, so I did.

As I talked, Grace hugged her pillow and held it tight as if she were a little girl at a sleepover. She sat almost without blinking and leaned in closer and closer as I told the sequence of events that led up to the kiss. When I finished, a smile spread across her face, and I couldn't really understand why. It wasn't exactly the time to smile.

"Why are you smiling?"

That wiped the smile off of her face. She hesitated to answer but, letting the smile return, said, "You're going to think that this is really weird, but there's this episode in the TV show that aired in the nineties—*Boy Meets World*—have you seen it?"

I didn't respond, so she continued, "What happens is just like your story. Basically, the show's lead, Cory, gets injured—not that you got injured—and then he has to stay in during the ski trip and ends up talking to the girl who works at the lodge—like Mark, not that Mark's a girl—so, anyway, they end up staying up all night talking, and then the ski lodge girl kisses him, and then Cory lies to Topanga, his girlfriend, and says nothing happened, but his best friend, Shawn, that's me I guess, knows and—" She looked up at my face to see how confused I was.

I wasn't in the mood for a TV show reference, especially when the only thing I could picture was a hurt look on Jack's face. "I haven't heard of the show," I said. "And this is my life."

"Sorry for rambling," she said.

"No, it's fine—"

She cut me off. "Anyway, I shouldn't be telling you about some TV show. I should be giving you advice on what to do, because that's what good friends do, right?"

I had been right. Grace was the kind of friend I thought she was, even though she was acting a little strange.

"You okay?" I asked, trying to sound casual.

"Yeah," she said, tracing her finger along the bedspread. "I'm just exhausted and drank too much coffee. I brought some coffee. Do you want some?"

"No, thanks." As appealing as it sounded to drink something that could wake me up, I could never stand the taste of coffee, no matter how much sugar or milk I added. I didn't want to change the subject too fast and be rude, but I needed her help. "Why would Mark do that?" I asked.

"Do what?" Grace said, giving me a blank stare. "Oh! Kiss you, you mean." She laughed. "Who knows. Mark is Mark. He'll do anything to break the rules or piss people off."

It hurt a little to hear that this drama that was blowing up so big in my mind could seem just like a game to Mark. But I remembered our last conversation and the last cryptic thing Mark had whispered in my ear, and I didn't think it was true that he didn't care about me at all.

Then I remembered Jack, and I needed Grace's advice on what I should do next, because I wasn't capable of figuring that out myself. "Should I tell Jack?" I asked.

"Honestly?" she asked. I nodded as she waited for an answer. "I don't think you should tell him. He's been through so much, and you just being Leanne 2.0 won't help him." As soon as the last part came out of her mouth, I could tell she wished she could take it back, but it was too late.

"What do you mean by Leanne 2.0?" I asked, hurt that everyone kept calling me that name, and by everyone, I meant Mark and now Grace.

"Sorry. It was stupid and mean. Forget I said anything. I just don't think Jack needs to be heartbroken again. He doesn't deserve it. He's a really good guy, you know. I mean, of course you know that, 'cause you're his . . . girlfriend, you know, so, obviously . . . sorry, I feel like I'm really high on coffee or something . . . just say something, or anything, really, so I'll stop talking."

I wasn't stupid. I knew something was going on with Grace, and I wanted to get to the bottom of it. I wanted her to blab just enough to let me find out what it was, but I hated seeing her like this, even if it had been a little funny at the beginning. I tried to think of something else to say to get her to stop talking. "I have a crush on Mark," I said. But, then again, maybe I was stupid.

Grace freaked out. "Wait—what? Would you mind repeating that, because I don't think I heard you correctly. You, Bella, good girl Bella, have a crush on bad boy Mark. Bella, you have a boyfriend. Why would—you kissed him, didn't you? Or at least you kissed him back, didn't you? Because if you did either of those things, you know Jack will literally kill you. He'll bring a knife and cut out your heart—" She stopped to look at my face, which was scared from the too-graphic images I wasn't ready for. "I think you get the idea," she said.

"Yeah . . . so I think I'm going to stay here until we have to head home at the end of the day. I really don't want to risk running into Jack or Mark. You go have fun, though, and if Jack asks how I'm doing, just tell him that I'm sick or something." The words came out too fast for me to think about what I was saying, but after replaying it in my head, it wasn't exactly a bad plan. I also doubted that Grace would let me stay alone in the room for hours with no company.

"Okay," Grace said, turning toward the door as if she were about to leave in her pajamas, so I started laughing like an idiot. She looked back at me, and for a millisecond I could've sworn I saw a look that was too dark for Grace to wear. It was gone before I could be sure whether it had ever been there and replaced by a smile. "I'm just kidding," she said, a second too late. It was as if she were saving herself. From what, though? I wasn't sure. I didn't let myself harp on the details too much because she was Grace, my best friend, the person I trusted the most. She was *my* Leanne 2.0—no, actually, she wouldn't have ditched me like Leanne did. I could still remember the look of hurt on Leanne's face after I'd hit her in the hallway, and even though the memory still bothered me, I pushed it out of my head and focused on my new best friend and the fun I was sure she'd make for me.

I was right about the fun. She turned on the TV, and we found a Pixar movie marathon. Grace had practically memorized all of the lines from *Toy Story* and *Frozen*, because those were the only movies we actually had time to watch before our bus was scheduled to leave. She spoke in funny voices and told me facts about the production of the movies that I wouldn't have known otherwise. I had no idea about this Pixar-nerd side of her, and for the rest of the day, it felt as though Grace was just being herself again.

123

Before I knew it, we were walking out of our room with our little suitcases. When we reached the lobby, Grace said she forgot something in the room, so I went on the bus without her. It didn't hit me until I was walking toward the back of the bus that I'd have to endure hours of sitting next to Jack while trying to keep from him the biggest secret I'd ever had. I didn't want to deal with sitting next to him, not saying anything for the entire ride again. The last time, at least both of us knew the reason we weren't talking. This time, I wouldn't talk, and he wouldn't know why. I could just tell him that I was sick, even though I wasn't and things were not okay. I wanted to believe everything was good, and the only way to do that was to make *him* believe that everything was good.

When I reached the back of the bus, I noticed Jack wasn't there yet. For some reason, I didn't even have to look to know. It was just the feel of the air, like some presence was missing. I considered for a moment whether to sit up front and talk to someone I hadn't spoken to in a while, but the first people who came to mind were my old friends, so I pushed the thought away. They weren't exactly whom I wanted to talk to, and they didn't provide a better alternative to sitting next to Jack. Standing in the middle of the bus, debating whether to go forward or back, I realized that I didn't really have anyone to confide in anymore, besides myself.

From outside, an unpleasantly familiar voice shouted, "Yo, Chicago!"

I looked out the window to see Mark standing in front of the ski lodge. The snow surrounding him was blinding white, and it took me a second to realize whom he was talking to. I surveyed Mark's surroundings until I realized that Jack had stopped on his way to the bus with his duffel bag slung over his shoulder.

"Asshole, I told you to stop calling me that," Jack said.

"Yo, Chicago, you left your AirPods in your room. House-keeping found them," Mark shouted, ignoring Jack's last comment. He held up his hand and waved the case in the air.

Jack made his way back to Mark, and it wasn't until they made physical contact that they were close enough for Mark to tell Jack what had happened between us — not that distance would've stopped him from shouting it all the way to the bus. Mark smiled in his devious way, and as Jack was about to take the AirPods, Mark snatched them away and held them up again in the air. Jack threw down his duffel bag and his backpack, and I prayed he wasn't going to punch Mark and get expelled. Just then, the front door opened, and Mark turned to see Grace come out and trip over Jack's bags. Mark tried to catch her but turned too fast, and they both ended up falling onto the fresh snow. I know it was mean to do, but I just looked away and pretended I didn't notice Grace falling. I couldn't bear to see Grace embar-rassed. I didn't think I'd ever seen her embarrassed before, and I wasn't really in the mood to make eye contact with Mark again. When I looked around for Jack, I couldn't find him. His bags were gone, and Grace and Mark had gotten up, brushing snow off their pants and gloves. I hoped Mark hadn't had a chance to tell Jack what had happened through the collision.

"Hey."

I turned to see Jack standing behind me, and I let out a deep breath that I didn't realize I was holding. He couldn't have been with Mark long enough to learn our secret. Jack smiled, and his eyes were too bright to have been told something dark and heart-breaking. We took our seats in the back of the bus, and Jack put his arm around me like he always had done. I guessed everyone was tired from the long day, because the back of the bus stayed quiet.

I closed my eyes and imagined that I stayed at the hot tub with Jack. I had fun and felt comfortable in my own skin. He told me that he loved me, not *Delphine*. His eyes lit up like they never had before, and they lit up for only me. I imagined that Leanne wasn't even in the hot tub to begin with. I imagined a world where Leanne didn't exist and neither did Mark. It was just me and Jack. That was it, and I loved it so much. As the bus pulled away from the ski lodge, I fell fast asleep in his arms.

"Hey, Bella, we're here." Why did he have to wake me up? I wished I could live in the perfect world I made for us forever.

"No, I wanna go back to sleep," I said. He laughed, but there was also an unsteadiness in his voice. Did someone tell him?

"Hey, can I talk to you? Just be serious for a minute," Jack said.

"I wasn't trying to be funny," I said, opening my eyes. It was already dark outside, and the inside of the bus was lit up by lights.

"Okay, fine, you were being serious. I was just thinking on the ride back that I don't know what happened last night, but I want to put it behind us. I don't think it's going to help us, so how about we just move on? Sound good?"

My thoughts raced. How did he know? Someone told him—or maybe I was jumping to conclusions. Jack never stated straight out what we were talking about. He could have finally realized his mistake at the hot tub and why I ran off.

"Bella?" He tried to meet my eyes with his, as if I'd fallen into a trance, and maybe I had. "Me and you. We're good, right?"

"You're not mad, right?" I asked.

"No, why would I be mad?" he asked. Maybe that meant he didn't know about what happened between Mark and me—unless Jack had a secret of his own, and each of our secrets canceled out the other. I didn't like the thought of Jack having a secret too, so I put on a smile.

"No reason," I said.

"Oh, before I forget, your phone has been ringing off the hook," Jack said.

I unzipped my backpack to take my phone out of the front pocket and followed Jack off the bus. We didn't have cell service in the mountains, and I got all my texts and calls from the weekend at once. They were all from my parents, and they had left me voicemails and sent me a bunch of texts about my grades — none of which were what I'd call positive. The school must have posted our grades right after we left for the ski trip. I'd forgotten about my grades during the trip because of all of the drama that was going on. Whoever chose when to send out grades was an evil genius. I checked my email, and sure enough, there was an unread message with the subject line: *REPORT CARDS*.

I knew I was about to encounter a whole new side of my mom. As I took my suitcase from the bottom of the bus, I decided to call my mom, who was probably already waiting in the school parking lot to pick me up. I thought it would be easier to call her first than to speak to her face-to-face, even though I had to see her in only a matter of minutes. I pressed the call button, and she answered after the first ring. "Hi, Mom," I said.

"I want you to break up with Jack Walker. Now."

Eleven

I'd never considered my relationship with my parents a good one, but it wasn't until I got a GPA of 2.34 that I really knew what that meant. Yes, I got a 2.34. I knew my grades were bad, but I didn't think they were *that* bad. Before I got a 2.34, I don't think I'd ever heard my parents yell at me so much. I know it was strange, since the average fifteen-year-old probably gets yelled at all of the time for doing stupid teenage things, but I'd never done those stupid teenage things until now.

On our car ride home, my mom sat in the driver's seat, and I opted to sit in the back, behind the passenger seat, to be as far away from her as possible. Even then, my mom was able to glare at me through the rearview mirror. I could tell she was burning with anger. She kept the radio off. The radio was never off in our car, since my parents liked to sing along to the latest chart-topper as if they were teenagers themselves. Instead, I could hear her breathing. The drive home felt like the longest five minutes I'd ever experienced.

When we got home, my dad was waiting for us in the living room. My dad always had something to say. He was the kind of person who stuck around to talk to someone *way* longer than he had to, who always had to give his opinion about an issue, even when no one asked. When I followed my mom into the house, I tried to avoid my dad by needing to carry my suitcase up the stairs. "Isabella Riley Carter, you better sit your ass down on this sofa right now!" he yelled. I left my suitcase at the foot of the stairs. I was shaking a little because I'd never heard my dad yell at me before. "You ungrateful little—"

"Michael!" My mom cut him off. I sat down on the sofa, and they stayed standing, looking down at me with their angry faces. I waited for them to shout their disappointment at me. My mom cleared her throat and said, "What your dad is trying to say is how can you do this Bella? How can you throw your future away over a stupid boy? We don't want to watch you do this to yourself." She had softened her voice rather than yelled, which was kind of nice, but that meant I'd actually have to answer.

"I don't know," I started to say, giving a stupid answer, because I couldn't think of anything else.

"Tell us, Bella, because we're trying—we're trying really hard to understand why you've done this to yourself," my dad said.

"I've done this to myself?" I asked.

"Your grades are your responsibility," my dad said. "Tell us, now, what has been going through your head."

"I don't know," I said again, because how could I ever explain myself to them when they never took the time to try to understand me? I couldn't bear my dad feeling the way he felt about me right then. I didn't want him to curse at me. I wanted it all to stop.

"Isabella Riley Carter, you better—"

"Because you don't care about me at all!" I shouted. "You have some fantasy about us being in the 'in-crowd' in society, and when I started making new friends, you both were happy for me.

Now all of a sudden, you care about my grades and tell me to break up with Jack? You're never paying attention!"

I'd never exploded like that to my parents, and as soon as I said what I did, I thought my dad would pick up a vase and throw it against the living room wall, like I remember him doing once after he'd lost a job a long time ago. Instead, I watched something shift in his eyes. The three of us stayed quiet. I couldn't handle them trying to comfort me and tell me that what I said wasn't true, because we all knew it was, so I got up and walked upstairs before they could think of something else to say to shift the mood.

I heard my mom calling after me, but when I closed my bedroom door, her voice downstairs became muffled. I wished my door was thick enough to mute my parents' voices altogether. I couldn't handle them calming down, only to have them come upstairs and start comparing their high school selves to me. I needed them to understand that I just wasn't them.

I didn't even realize I was crying until I tasted a salty tear on my lips. I walked over to the standing mirror across from my bed, because there had always been something oddly comforting about watching myself cry. I wasn't exactly sure what the comforting part was, though. It was something Leanne and I had done when we were kids: whenever we cried about something, she'd take me to the mirror, and we'd look into our crying faces and then burst out laughing. We could never really remember what we were crying about in the first place. When I asked Leanne why she thought looking into the mirror was helpful, she just shrugged and gave a vague answer that was somehow satisfying, just like every other time I asked her a question she didn't know how to answer.

Looking into my red face in the mirror alone, I saw how much of an ugly crier I was. I stared at myself for a while, letting this girl I barely recognized cry. I wanted to figure out how I'd gotten the girl I was looking at into this mess. The easiest thing would be to say that it was all Jack's fault. Everyone else seemed to be blaming every bad thing I did on him, so why not me too? But deep down, I wouldn't settle for that easy answer because I knew the cause of what was happening was more than just Jack.

What was pushing me to be that person whom Jack liked? Or maybe the real question was *who* was pushing me to change who I was? Had Leanne defined the type of person Jack liked and who I thought I should be? Throughout our friendship and up until now, I'd always compared myself to Leanne, and so had everyone else, but truthfully, we were nothing alike. I had always thought that by some miracle, we would be able to keep balancing each other out to the point where we would always stay best friends. Now, we'd barely talked at all in over a year, and I wondered whether there was a part of me that was trying to be like her, to make up for the fact that she was out of my life. I didn't know the answer, but in thinking about Leanne, I also wondered whether she had somehow defined how all of this drama was going to turn out. Was she the one who made it some sort of destiny for me to end up screwing up my relationship with Jack too?

No, I didn't want to think that. Maybe Mark had this image that I was just like Leanne, but *I* was the one who made the decision to talk to him in the first place. I was the one who decided what I wanted to say. I was the one who gave him the chance to kiss me, so maybe in some weird, twisted way . . . it really was my fault? Even though I didn't want to admit that I had at least a part in what had happened, it made me feel that I had some control in the situation, rather than believing that everything bad had just happened to me. I suddenly realized why looking at the mirror was so helpful. It allowed me to see a bigger picture and to look at myself with new eyes.

"Hey, Bells, can I come in?" My mom knocked on the door. She was probably trying to be the good cop in some good cop/bad cop routine. I didn't fall for it, because as much as she would try to hide it, I knew she was still angry that I'd screwed up.

Before she gave me the chance to answer, like always, she walked in. Even though I'd stopped crying, my face was still tear drenched and blotchy, and I wished she would have just stayed outside and not felt like she had to pretend to be warm and comforting.

"Your dad and I had talked with your principal right after we got your report card, and we all decided that it would best if we sat down for a meeting in his office." I knew she wasn't asking for my opinion, but I just had to say something.

"No, thanks."

"I wasn't asking for your opinion."

In my head I thought, called it. "I really don't want to go."

"Why?"

"Because I can't sit in a room where all three of you are going to hate me and blame all of my problems on Jack." The sentence came out more bluntly than I wanted it to. I told myself to keep my lips sealed and lock them with a key, but that didn't seem to work.

"Hon, we don't hate you. We're trying to help you after you made some mistakes. We're going to ask your teachers for as much extra credit as possible to boost your grades and—"

"No, thanks," I repeated. I didn't need that. What I did need was for my mom to leave me alone and let me wallow in my misery. I needed her to let me just live with the consequences of the present moment, even though I knew there was no chance of that happening.

"Listen to me, Isabella. You're going to this meeting, and we're going to figure out what the hell is going on with you."

"Get out!" I'd rarely ever been this angry in my life, but I hated that my mom thought she knew what she was talking about when she didn't.

"Don't talk to me that way!" I'd never seen my mom so angry at me, and it was an ugly look on her. I cared for only a fraction of a second until tears started streaming down my cheeks again.

I knew that she was my mom and she'd seen me cry before, but still, I didn't want her to see me as an emotional wreck. I knew we were supposed to be close and all, especially since she was on the younger side. But the older I grew, the more far apart I felt from her, to the point where I'd given up on a close relationship between us altogether. The worst part was it wasn't even all her fault, because I knew she'd tried to find some common interests between us at some point. We were just too different.

I looked up at my mom's face, which was still masked with that same ugly anger, and I wanted to say sorry or to at least apologize in some form, but I couldn't say the words. After looking at me for another few long seconds, she said, "I just wanted to tell you that the meeting is tomorrow at 7:00, so you'll have to wake up early so we can get there on time."

Then she left. For just a second, I wanted her to care a little more, to stay in the room with me and yell and scream. But then I realized that if she cared even a little more, I'd probably be grounded or something. I wished everything was different, and I wished I could be close with and talk to my mom, but I couldn't. So I let her leave and went to bed.

"Bella, wake up!"

"For God's sake, you better wake up right now! You are the reason we called this meeting, and you won't be the reason we're late!"

I opened my eyes to see my parents towering over me with nothing but anger on their faces . . . so nothing had changed from last night.

"I'm up," I said. "I'm up."

"Did you not set your frickin' alarm?" My dad was past the point of being just angry. He turned to my mom. "See, Gia, I told you this would happen. If you just came in like I told—"

"Michael, please, just shut up, because if you stand here and keep talking, we're going to be late."

My dad turned to leave, and my mom followed him, so I pushed myself off of my bed. I walked over to my closet, and, for the first time in forever, I pulled out a sweatshirt and leggings without second-guessing what I was wearing or even caring about how I looked. I was done with trying to impress people. I was a failure.

I got ready in under five minutes and went downstairs. I didn't even bother with breakfast, because it wasn't like I could eat when I had no appetite or energy. I walked over to the car, where my parents had been sitting for five minutes, but the looks they shot at me made it seem like they had been waiting for hours. We were already late to the meeting, so did a few more minutes really matter?

We were quiet during the car ride. I had taken my parents singing along to the chart-toppers for granted. I'd always thought it was annoying, but as I stared out the window at the houses passing by, I thought it wouldn't hurt for them to turn on the radio. I didn't want to be left alone with my thoughts. I tried to focus on the eerie silence, but what was the point when it was just that—silence?

I was grateful that the drive wasn't more than five minutes. I didn't think any of us would have survived cooped up together for any longer. Mainly, my dad would have burst out yelling from all of the anger that was bubbling inside of him. Once the car stopped, I jumped out. Then I wondered when I had ever been so eager to get out of the car to go to the principal's office. My choices in that moment on where to go next seemed to be lose-lose all around. I couldn't stay in the car, obviously, and I was about to walk into yet another situation where someone was about to tell me how I was a failure.

When I walked into the school with my parents, I expected there to be fewer people wandering around than there actually were. I guessed people were busy with early extracurricular meetings, which was a foreign idea to me. I wasn't that into extra-curriculars, but other people must have really liked them, at least enough to roll out of bed early on a Monday morning. People were staring at me, and I wasn't really sure why—was it ridiculous that I was at school early? It took me a second to remember that my parents were trailing behind me. The principal's office was at the other end of the long hall, and it seemed that the students were lined up against the lockers, staring at us. I could imagine the things that were going on in their heads—especially the rumors they were about to spread—but I ignored everyone's stares, or I tried to anyway, because I had bigger worries ahead.

When we entered the principal's office, I thought about the last time I had been in there. It was when Jack was sitting beside me, when the principal suspended us. I didn't think that I'd actually wind up in his office again for a meeting with my parents. Now there he was, sitting behind his desk and smiling way too much for how terrible the situation was that brought us there. For some reason, as my mom and I sat down, the principal and my dad shook hands and made small talk about "the old days." I didn't care about how embarrassing this situation was as much as I thought I would.

During the meeting, I tuned out. What was the point of sitting in the principal's office for twenty minutes as he told me everything I was doing wrong with my life? I didn't need him to tell me I was a failure at life without being able to say it outright. The principal mostly talked to my parents and glanced at me from time to time, which was my signal to nod and say, "Yeah." I didn't need him to tiptoe around me as though I were some good little girl who was going through a phase. Why couldn't people just understand that maybe this was who I was and the "good little girl" thing was actually the phase? What if I wasn't this angel that people could put a crown on and call a cute little princess?

The principal and my parents didn't understand who I was. They didn't know the real me. Why couldn't they just understand that maybe the quiet thing was an act because I was afraid of the real me and about what other people would think? But that was before. That was when people thought I was someone I was not. I was afraid they'd run away screaming when they found out I had an actual voice, thoughts, and opinions. I had even tried to run away from myself, but that was before. Now I had to run away from the people who pretended to know me. Maybe they pretended enough to the point where they actually believed they did, but I didn't buy any of this crap they were saying to help me "get back on track" for a second.

When we walked out of the office, the principal had given me a flyer that advertised after-school tutoring, which I knew I wasn't going to go to. Our meeting achieved nothing but seemed to have made my parents feel better. Already, my dad was looking at his cell phone and checking out of what happened, and my mom and I stepped into the girls' restroom. "We have a lot to talk about when we get home," my mom said, and I stared at myself in the mirror as she disappeared into one of the stalls.

I wanted to burst into tears, but I wouldn't let that happen while my mom was still around. Was it normal that all of those thoughts occupied my brain during the meeting? I stared at myself in the mirror and wondered whether what people were thinking about me was actually true. I wondered whether being a failure, when it came down to it, was really all my fault.

The restroom door opened, and just my luck, Bea walked in. It was terrible timing to see her when I was vulnerable and at my worst. We looked at each other, and I bet she never felt the way that I did. I bet she could say whatever was on her mind all the time. I bet people didn't judge her, and when she did something different, people would just follow her as though she'd started a trend.

"Oh, what could you possibly be crying about?" Bea asked. "Boy troubles?"

"No, actually." I didn't realize I was crying, and I wiped a tear away from my cheek. I was suddenly aware of my mom only a few feet away from us behind a stall, so I put a finger to my lips.

Bea lowered her voice to a whisper. "Why?"

I didn't have time to answer her before the toilet flushed and my mom came out of the restroom stall. Her eyes landed on Bea. "Oh, hi, Bea," my mom said, turning on the sink to wash her hands,

"Hi, Gia, how are you?" It was weird to see Bea acting polite.

"I'm good. I just saw your mom the other day at pilates. She says you're getting interested in photography?" I forgot sometimes that my mom was friends with Bea's mom, even though my mom was almost fifteen years younger than hers.

Bea shrugged. "Just one of my passing interests. We'll see where it goes." I cringed.

"That's great," my mom said. She took a paper towel and dried her hands. "Bella, we'll finish our conversation when you get home." Then, to my surprise, she gave me a quick hug. "Oh, honey, school is about to start, and your dad needs the car to go to work. I'll say my goodbyes now." She gathered me in her arms for one second, and I could smell the sweetness of her perfume. She walked out before I had the chance to say anything more.

When it was just Bea and me in the bathroom, I turned to her and said sorry, even though I wasn't really sure what I was apologizing for.

"What was that about?"

"I basically failed art and English and got Cs and Ds in all of my other classes, so I just had a meeting with the principal and my parents." I was surprised that I was being so open with Bea and telling her everything that just happened. As a joke, I added, "It was dumb, but I might start bawling my eyes out."

"Don't," Bea said, laughing. "I thought you were supposed to be smart."

"Yeah, me too," I said.

Bea laughed again. "You know, you're not as bad as I thought you were." I knew she would remember. She must have read the look on my face, since she added, "That was the last thing you said to me; remember?"

"Oh, right," I said, even though, of course, I remembered. "Sorry about that."

Bea shrugged and looked into the mirror, checking out her brows. "Apology accepted. So you think everything is going to work out okay with your mom?"

"I don't know," I sighed. "My parents are being such a pain."

Bea stared at me through the mirror. "You've got to be kidding me. *You* have parent problems? I bet your problems are nothing compared to mine."

"You actually have problems?" I asked with just the right amount of sarcasm.

"Very funny," she answered back with the same amount, which didn't convince me. "You don't believe me?"

"Not really."

She turned to face me. Maybe it was because I had just told her honestly about how my own life was falling apart or because she saw my mom just a minute before, but something had opened up between us, and I could tell Bea wanted to tell me something important about herself.

"How about this?" she asked. "Do you have any idea what it's like to live with people who will judge you if you tell them who you really are? Do you know how hard it is to pretend you're this person you're not? Do you know what it's like to hear your parents talking about people just like you, as if they have a mental problem or an instability, at your freaking dinner table, right in front of you, but all you can do is smile and nod as you realize that all of the things they've just said are about you? Do you know what it's like to know that once I say two words, their image of me will change forever?"

It was a nice speech and all, and I could relate with some of the things she mentioned, but she never actually said what she was talking about. I also thought Bea couldn't have problems I could understand from my own life, because she was Bea—the mighty and impenetrable Queen Bee-atch-rix—so I told her, "I don't get it." After I heard myself, I thought I sounded stupid.

Bea took a breath. She looked back at herself in the mirror and ran a hand through her hair. "I know you may have thought that I was jealous of you and Jack," she said. I didn't know how she was paying attention to things that I had never said out loud or how she seemed to be a mind reader like Mark. "But that's not true," she continued. "Because I'm not attracted to guys."

"What?" I asked.

She looked up in the mirror and met her own eyes. Then she met mine and said, "I'm gay."

"Oh," I said. That probably wasn't my best moment, but as I replayed everything she had just said to me about her parents ranting at their dinner table, her story began making sense.

She threw her head back and laughed, relieved. "Yeah, wow! I did not think you'd be the first person I would come out to," she said.

"Wait, you haven't told anyone, and all of a sudden you decided to tell me? I mean, we're not even friends — I mean, I'm not really sure what you call this." I felt a little bad about saying that last part out loud, but I was a little confused about what to say. I'd never been in this kind of situation before.

"Well, you hate me anyway already, so why not?"

"Bea, I don't hate you." It was true. The more I talked to Bea, the more I liked her. Maybe it was because when it was just the two of us, she didn't have to act the least bit phony and I could see that she actually had normal human problems. I wasn't really sure how we were warming up to each other, when Bea was the last person I thought I'd become friends with, but I did know one thing: the nickname Leanne and I gave her was kind of mean — no, it *was* mean — and Bea didn't deserve it.

"Then why do you always treat me like I'm the villain?" she asked.

"I don't treat you like —" I paused to look at her face and saw how she wasn't buying it. "Okay, fine. I did always think you were jealous of Jack and me, but obviously that wasn't the case. Wait; I'm confused. Why are you always talking with the girls about hookup gossip and guys at school? And didn't you date a senior last year?" The question had been wandering in my head for a while before I even realized it was there. I remembered now how Bea had a popular older boyfriend right when we got to high school and how that put her at the top of the social map right away.

"Oh, that guy," Bea said, rolling her eyes. "He asked me out, you know, even though I told everyone it was me. I was, what, fourteen then? I was confused about who I was, just like everyone else. About the talk with the girls . . ." She paused, and for a second, her face looked uncomfortable. Then she smoothed out her expression and said, "For a long time I was trying to convince myself I was someone I'm not."

"I could relate to you on that," I said. "Sometimes I wonder who I am when I'm with Jack . . . whether that's the real me or whether that's someone I'm trying to convince myself I want to be."

Bea laughed. "Oh, Jack," she said. "Somehow he always finds himself in girl troubles. For the record, Jack's like a brother to me. We've known each other forever, but he's just so sensitive, especially after the whole divorce. I didn't want to hurt his feelings, but when you and Jack started dating, I was suspicious."

"Suspicious?"

"More like protective, I guess. I thought that it would always be him and Leanne. Leanne and I were friends when the two of them started dating, and I remember thinking how Leanne is, or was, perfect for him." Everything clicked, but something was still bothering me.

"She's not dead, you know," I said.

"What?" Bea asked.

"Oh, it's just that people usually do that 'is/was' thing for dead people." As soon as I said it, I realized I ruined the conversation.

141

"Sorry, it was just that they were really good together," she said, shouldering her bag and turning toward the door to leave. "I don't mean to be rude, but she really shouldn't have broken them up."

"Who?"

Bea opened the door right before I could get an answer from her, but I was ninety-nine percent sure she was talking about how Leanne had ruined their relationship, so it didn't really matter much that Bea didn't answer the question. "You wouldn't be the worst friend to have," she said. "Later."

"Yeah," I said, not sure about how else to answer. For a minute, I stood in the bathroom by myself and tried to think whether I'd ever had a stranger conversation or a stranger morning, for that matter. The first bell rang to get to class, and after the meeting at the principal's office, there was no way I could get into any more trouble or be late.

I ran to my locker, and there was Jack, waiting for me. "Bella?" he said.

"Oh no." I couldn't really deal with him right now. I still needed hours to process everything that had happened, and school hadn't even started yet. "Hey, Jack," I said, hoping he didn't hear that first part.

"What did you just say?"

"Nothing. It doesn't matter," I lied, because I couldn't burden him with my problems.

"Bella, we need to talk."

"We do?"

"Yeah, how did it go with your parents last night?"

Before I knew it, I was ranting. "They hate me. They came for a meeting this morning, and it was . . . they're just so mad at me, Jack. You should've seen my dad. He was so freaking scary. If you had been there, you wouldn't have even recognized him and—" Suddenly, it hit me. Mark kissed me, and I still didn't tell Jack, which made me conscious that I was actively keeping something from him. Did Jack know what happened? Was he playing with my mind in an attempt to get the truth out of me? Was he going to accuse me of lying to him? Was he going to accuse me of letting Mark kiss me? Was he going to tell me it was all my fault?

"Bella?" He knew. He definitely knew. The second bell rang that signaled we should already be in class. We were both late.

"I've gotta go," I said.

"Wait, Bella. I'm not done talking to you." He knew. That was what he wanted to talk to me about, wasn't it?

On the small chance he didn't know, I couldn't tell him. I knew that if I looked him in the eyes, I'd somehow manage to give it all away. I couldn't crush him, and that meant not leaving, but if I stayed and dared to look him in the eye, I'd hurt him either way. "I—"

I felt an arm wrap around me, and it wasn't Jack's. "She has to go because we're already late for class. Oh, and before I forget, Jack, you're coming for dinner tonight, right?"

"Right," he said distantly, trying to pretend he wasn't just as shocked as I was at Bea's friendly gesture.

"Wait a sec. I didn't know you two were, like, actual friends. I mean, I just thought—"

"We've gotta go," Bea said, interrupting him. It was official: Bea was my new hero.

We walked down the hall, and when we were out of earshot from Jack, I said, "Thanks. You didn't need to do that for me."

"Yeah, I did. I was serious about that friend thing a few minutes ago, and you looked like you really needed saving. Besides, you're the first person I've come out to. Shouldn't that count for something? I wouldn't have told you if I thought you were a complete jerk, like some other people at this school."

I almost laughed, because for the longest time I thought that she was a complete Queen Bee-atch, but if she was serious about being friends, I had to be serious about it too. We stopped walking a few feet from Ms. Anderson's door.

"Hey, um, Bea, I need to tell you something."

"Yeah, I'm listening."

"You remember at the ski lodge when I ran out of the hot tub? Well, then I forgot my room key, and I thought someone would catch me out in the hall, but it was only—"

"What's your point?" Bea cut me off. She was always straightforward, and there was no way of getting out of telling her now.

"Yeah, sorry."

"Don't apologize; just tell me." It wasn't rude the way she said it. It was if she cared.

"Mark kissed me," I said bluntly.

"That little—how could she do this?" Bea said under her breath, but I could tell it came out louder than intended.

"What?" Her reaction made no sense.

"How could he do this, I mean. How could Mark do that to you?"

"Wait, so you're not going to run off and tell Jack?"

"No, Bella, I was dead serious about being real friends with you. I know it wasn't your fault. Besides, you've gotta have someone in your corner."

"Great, so now I have you and Grace in my corner." I didn't have to finish the sentence to realize that it was awkward. I knew they weren't the best of friends, and I was just going to have to deal with that.

"Hey, Bella, I need to tell you something really important."

"Yeah, sure, anything," I said as I tried to come up with an idea to take back my last comment, which clearly made the friendship between Bea and me more awkward than it was already.

"It's about you and—"

"Ms. Carter?"

I turned to see Ms. Anderson standing at the door of her classroom.

"Can it wait? I've gotta go," I said, running into the classroom. I didn't have a chance to let Bea finish her sentence, and I'd be lying if I said I wasn't the least bit curious to know what she wanted to tell me.

Twelve

Someone kept texting me, and I tried to ignore it, especially since I was in Ms. Anderson's class. It seemed as if every day gave her another excuse to hate me. After not glancing to check who was texting me the past three times, I finally gave in. It was Grace. Now, that was a complicated subject. Two weeks had passed since my conversation with Bea in the girls' bathroom. Time flew by since then.

There were reasons I did want to answer each time Grace texted or called. I wanted to answer because she was my friend, but the problem was that now Bea was also my friend. What I didn't realize before was that Grace wasn't quiet because of her personality—it was because there was unspoken beef between her and Bea that neither of them was willing to speak to me about. I knew that whatever was going on between them wasn't over some stupid jealous rage over a crush, obviously, but rather seemed bigger and more important. Every time I tried to ask either of them about it, they managed to shift the conversation away from the topic, and it was only after our conversation ended that I would realize I'd been played.

I didn't like being the middle person in their fight, or whatever they wanted to call the thing that was going on between them. It was hard enough splitting up my time between the two of them *and* Jack, even though I hadn't actually talked to Jack much in the past two weeks. During the time I wasn't involved in some Bea vs. Grace drama, I had to focus on my schoolwork. I made a deal with my parents that if I put in more effort at school, they would let me be more independent like they used to. And that was only after I convinced them that Jack wasn't the problem, even though there was a part of me that didn't believe that.

I blamed my lack of focus on Grace instead. It was a spur-of-the-moment thing. I knew my parents wanted to place the blame on someone, but I couldn't let it be me or Jack. I didn't want to ruin some idealized version they had of him. I also couldn't place the blame on Bea because, well, my mom loved her, and she wouldn't stop talking about her the way she did when Leanne suddenly became popular. As much as I hated it, I needed to please my parents to have my sixteenth birthday party, and it didn't matter how I did it or whom I hurt.

When my parents told me they didn't want me to hang out with Grace anymore, their voices and expressions were so different from when they had tried to blame Jack. They didn't know Grace, and they seemed to be glad that she was the one they told me not to hang out with anymore, rather than someone like Jack or Bea, who had gained their stamp of approval. That was fine by me. My parents were happy, and I only had to pretend I wasn't hanging out with Grace anymore. I just told them I was hanging out with Bea all the time, which provided the perfect cover. Each time I lied to them, I swore I wouldn't use my friendship with Bea to my advantage, but I found myself doing exactly that again and again.

To be honest, though, my relationship with my parents hadn't exactly improved. We just went back to the same relationship we had before the whole bad grades drama. When I actually showed up to after-school tutoring and started pulling up my grades again, we had an unspoken agreement to just put a blanket over the whole situation. I knew how the blanket would stay over our real issues for long enough that it would seem almost nonexistent, which is how my parents preferred things to be. I knew how my parents were, and I talked to them only when necessary, so eventually we just fell back into our normal routine.

Grace's texts were questions about what I was going to do after school. I ignored them and forced my attention back to history class, because when I was in that classroom, I had to act like a stellar student. Otherwise, Ms. Anderson might send me to the principal's office again, in which case my life would probably fall apart. Anyway, Grace was starting to really get on my nerves. She was being clingy and annoying, and it was downright irritating. I thought she was just really jealous of my friendship with Bea, and why would I have any reason to think it was anything else?

When class ended, I proceeded with the routine I had developed over the past two weeks. I had to go the long way to my next class to avoid both Grace's locker and Bea's locker. I walked quickly with my head down and looked at my shoes, which was how most kids walked through the halls, except they were staring at their phones. I tried to blend in with them so that anyone who might notice me wouldn't suspect that I was trying to avoid someone.

"Hey, Bella, wait up!" It was Jack. It was always Jack, popping up at the most inconvenient times. He was going to ruin my perfectly thought-out method for getting to my next class unnoticed.

I turned around and watched him walk toward me. He was wearing his usual yellow basketball shoes. Jack still didn't know what happened between Mark and me at the ski lodge, and even though I hoped I'd forget about it as time went on, I only felt more and more guilty. At first, I did try to tell Jack what happened. I tried to make opportunities to tell him, but when a moment opened up between us when we were alone and quiet, I could never bring myself to tell him. I kept making up excuses. Then I woke up one day and realized that a week and a half had passed, and it was, in fact, too late. I never did tell Jack, and the guilt was eating me up inside.

Somehow, I managed to push it away and muster up a smile whenever I talked to him, but maybe it was because of guilt that I avoided him more and more. I thought about how things could have been worse if Mark still went to our school. I couldn't imagine what it would be like if Mark were around and showed up at the most random times to remind me of what happened. Honestly, Mark probably would have told Jack about it by now, but thankfully, he wasn't here in person and didn't have a chance.

I took a deep breath to stop myself from going further down this spiral of thoughts. Nothing had even happened to make Jack suspect anything . . . at least not to my knowledge. I had to push away my guilt when I talked to him so that he wouldn't suspect anything.

"How's the party planning going?" he asked. In all the anxiety I had about classes, Bea, Grace, Jack, and Mark, I had almost forgotten about my sweet sixteen birthday party happening that weekend. It had been Bea's idea to throw one, and after I agreed, she took over all the planning.

"Good," I said. To be honest, the party prep probably was going pretty okay. I just wasn't spending as much time on it as I wanted to—it was all Bea. It was like she had a superpower; she actually knew exactly what I wanted without me having to say anything.

"So I'll be at your place at 7:00 tonight?"

"Right, right," I said, distantly. My thoughts were still in a jumble, and I didn't want to confuse Jack and say that I thought today was Thursday, not Friday. I didn't tell him that although at first I thought my party started at 8:00, he was right in that it really started at 7:00. "You know what—I really have to go to class," I said.

"Bella!" Bea called out from down the hall.

Was it guilt that made me so paranoid? Over the past month, Bea and I had become close friends, but as I turned to look at her, I couldn't help but play out every possible scenario of what could happen if she betrayed me. She smiled as she approached us, and I imagined that smile morphing again into a Queen Bee-atch-rix laugh as she yelled, "Hey, Jack! You're talking to the new sophomore slut!" I thought about Leanne and how she'd had to put up with people calling her that name behind her back all year and how much it must have hurt her. There was an afternoon when I was over at Bea's house and she was showing me different pictures of balloon arrangements we could have at my party, and I asked her why she called Leanne that name with the girls. Bea had to pause to think about it, and she said that even though she knew it was a mean thing to do, it was easy to get the girls to gang up on someone.

When Bea caught up with Jack and me, my heart was beating in my throat. I knew it wasn't like our lives were at stake or anything if she betrayed me. But in thinking about Leanne again, I realized I was tired of losing friends I cared about. Bea also was someone I had just become friends with and didn't want to lose anytime soon.

"You wanna walk to class together? I have a bunch of things to tell you about the party," Bea said. As she stood beside me, she became a real person again, someone whom I laughed with and talked to, and it was strange how easy it was for me to morph my friends into people they weren't in my head.

"Sure," I said, shaking off any bad thoughts I'd had about Bea.

"Good." We said bye to Jack, and Bea started to walk away before I could even register what was happening. I sped-walked to catch up to her, and when I did, I found her pace and matched her steps—something I got used to doing by now.

As Bea started talking about the details of my party that I really had no clue about, I thought about how Bea was protective of me and how it was nice and refreshing to have someone looking out for me, because no one had been that good a friend to me since Leanne—not even Jack, and that's if I wanted to call him my friend. There was Grace too, but she was a different kind of protective. Different how? I couldn't quite put my finger on it, and I didn't need to—at least, not quite yet.

"Bella!" Grace approached us from down the hall. Just another surprise to ruin my plan.

"Perfect," Bea said to me. I knew that it was just one word that might have sounded silly and simple, but I was starting to get good at speaking and understanding "teenage girl." I know I'm a teenage girl, but I never quite mastered the art of saying something to disguise what I really meant, and I never really had to until now. Bea gave me a look that translated to: *She had better not be involved in planning this thing. You're lucky I agreed to invite her at all.*

"Grace!" Bea exclaimed when Grace approached us, with just the right amount of sarcasm in her voice that I almost smiled— that is, until I realized that I was the one who was making things worse between them.

"Hey, Bells," Grace said, completely ignoring Bea as she shoved her way in between us. She'd been calling me by that nickname ever since the one time she came over to my house and overheard my mom calling me that. I didn't have the heart to tell her that that's what Leanne used to call me, ever since sixth grade when we went on our Philadelphia trip. We had played a secret game of truth or dare during the tour of the Liberty Bell, which ended with Leanne daring me to touch it while she came up with some distraction. While I attempted to touch the bell, Leanne raised her hand to ask the tour guide something, and for the first time ever she blanked and got nervous, so she started mumbling, "Bells . . . Bells . . . Bells . . . Bella . . . Bells," and at that moment everyone turned to see me trying to reach the Liberty Bell with my short eleven-year-old arm.

I got scolded by our teacher, and Leanne, being Leanne, found the whole thing hilarious and started calling me "Bells, Bells, Bells, Bella, Bells." Eventually, the name got shortened to Bella Bells, until it was just Bells. My mom overheard the nickname and liked it, so she started calling me Bells too. I didn't want to tell my mom the story about how I'd gotten in trouble, or tell her that it was Leanne's nickname for me and not hers, so it stuck. I didn't need to go through all of that with Grace, mostly because I didn't think she'd have the patience. It seemed everything was about Grace vs. Bea lately.

"Hey, Grace, I'm walking with Bella, so I'll see you around, 'kay?" Bea said, which, in "teenage girl speak," meant: *Hey, Grace, I'm walking with Bella — not you — so you better watch your back and hope I don't see you trying to steal her from me, got it?*

Grace smiled, and in teenage girl speak it was really like giving Bea the middle finger. In a sweet voice, Grace said, "It's fine; I have class right next to Bella's anyway, so it's not out of my way at all. Hey, don't you have chemistry right now? You do know that's on the other side of the building, right?" That meant: *Not gonna work for me. Bella's my friend, and you better get the hell out of my way. Bella was my friend first, and in case you haven't realized,*

I don't like you. You better get far away from us and go back to wherever the hell you came from.

I know it seemed really bad for me to just stand there and not do anything. They were at each other's throats while smiling at each other, and I heard what they were really saying. I just didn't know what to do, and I didn't want to ruin either friendship. I'd barely spoken to my real best friend in two years, and there these girls were, both of whom I could call my good friends, fighting over me. I was finally getting over Leanne, and I was happy.

"I'm telling you: hair up will look much better with that dress."

Bea had been "helping" me get ready, and by helping, I mean she was doing everything but physically putting me in the dress. She watched from my chair in the corner of my room, and it was just at the right angle so that I could see her as I looked at myself in the mirror. I always wore my hair down and had been arguing that for the past ten minutes at least, but as I held my hair up, I could tell Bea was right.

"Fine, do what you want. I'm done fighting with you on this," she said with a sly smile, and I knew she knew what I was thinking. Even though I had no intention of admitting that she'd won, I reluctantly tied my hair up. "You could look a little happier about it, you know," Bea said.

I gave her a smile, which was fake and on command, but there was some realness behind it, which we both knew. When she was quiet for too long, I turned around to see that something was on her mind—probably just another thing she wanted me to fix.

"What is it now?" I asked.

"You're not going to like it," Bea said without giving much of an answer.

"Let me guess. You want me to put on a different dress, but we can't do that because it's already—"

"No, it's not about that," Bea said. Then she seemed to change her mind again, which was unlike her. Bea was always decisive, and even though she could shrug off whatever thought was on her mind in that moment, I wouldn't let it go that easily.

"Then what is it?"

"It's nothing."

"Okay, you don't get to do that. You never start telling me something and then change your mind." Right at that moment, I remembered that thing she wanted to tell me outside of Ms. Anderson's classroom, right before I had to run inside and didn't let her finish. I was starting to wish that we hadn't been interrupted and she could have told me whatever it was that she knew. Then maybe we wouldn't be in that situation right then and there.

"It's about Grace. You're not going to like it," she said. "You know how she's always carrying around that notebook? She's not—I don't trust her and neither should you. Just listen to me, okay? She—"

"Knock, knock. Is there a birthday girl in here?" Jack opened my bedroom door. I should have been happy that Jack arrived at my party early, which is what I would've expected of him, but instead I was irritated that he'd interrupted Bea and me. We turned to him, and I thought that what he said was probably the corniest thing he'd ever said to me. That got me thinking about anything else he could have said that was corny, which meant that my thoughts had shifted away from the conversation Bea and I were having. The moment was ruined for what Bea had to tell me—again.

Jack came over to me and wrapped his arm around my waist. He carried a little gift bag in his hand, and I couldn't help but peek inside. There was a bunch of pink tissue paper, which I hoped didn't conceal jewelry. I'd never been big on jewelry, and I hoped that Jack knew me well enough to know that, despite the fact that I was presently covered in earrings, bracelets, and necklaces from Bea's prized jewelry box. "Hey, Jack, tell Bella how good she looks with her hair up," Bea said.

"You look really pretty," Jack said, as he noticed me peeking into the bag. He must have noticed my expression, because he said, "Hey, don't give up on me so easily. It's not what you think." He handed me the bag.

I dug through the pink tissue paper to find a white gift card that I almost missed, as it blended in with the white gift bag. I took it out and flipped it over to see a handwritten gift card for Tony's, most likely written by Tony himself, since it would have been nearly impossible for Jack's handwriting to be that neat.

I looked up at him, and it wasn't until he smiled that I realized I had been smiling so much that my mouth was starting to hurt. Still, I could tell he was waiting for a response. I wanted to tell him that he'd given me one of the sweetest, most thoughtful birthday presents I had ever gotten. Even though it was a gift card, it meant so much to me, because it brought us back to the beginning of our relationship when we'd hardly known each other, when everything felt fresh, exciting, and brand new. For some reason, I couldn't get the words out of my mouth. Something was stopping me, and all I managed to say was a quiet thank you.

"You're welcome, but just wait till midnight tonight, because that's not even the best present I have to give to you. You have to wait until your actual birthday for that."

All I could do was smile like an idiot. I couldn't manage to form any words yet again — I couldn't even muster a "thank you."

Bea sensed something was wrong. Even though I wasn't sure yet what that was, she looked over at Jack and asked, "Can you go see if anyone's here yet? And, oh, while you're at it, can you try to make sure no one brought any booze?"

"Yeah," Jack said. He sounded disappointed, and maybe he was starting to sense something wrong too, but he left before I could be sure.

Bea closed the bedroom door and turned to me with a serious expression on her face. "What's up?"

"I don't know. I just feel like I can't talk to him anymore. Ever since . . . the ski trip, I guess."

"You feel guilty about the Mark thing?" It was the first time she had brought up Mark since I told her what happened.

"Maybe. I just feel awful and like I can't do what Leanne did to Jack. The way she hurt him — "

"Forget Leanne for a minute. How do you feel?" That was the best thing she could have said to me, because it helped to take me out of my head and into my heart.

I thought for a moment. "I want to tell him. I don't want to pretend or lie anymore."

"Okay. Tell him tonight."

"But it's my — "

"Oh, come on, Bella. We both know that you're going to end up pushing this off if you don't tell him now," Bea said. I knew she was right.

"Okay, tonight." I paused for a minute because I almost forgot where Jack was. "Do you think Jack is going to do what you said about the no-alcohol thing? Because my parents will probably draw the line at that point."

"Yeah, I trust him. He's like all anti-alcohol because of his dad and hates how it can transform you into this whole other person, like a monster. He wrote a whole epic poem about it once and won a prize. Anyway, what I'm trying to say is, yeah, I trust him."

Why did that have to make Jack seem more attractive? Why couldn't Bea have made it easier for me and said that Jack was a monster, or anything else that would have made it even a little bit easier for me to tell him the truth? In the end, though, telling the truth would be the easy part—it would be getting through all the lies, and the whys behind the lies, that would be hard.

We could hear music start playing from downstairs. "You wanna get to the party?" I asked Bea, and without answering, she walked out of my room, so I took that as an answer and followed her down the steps.

When I got downstairs, I was surprised to see that just five minutes after 7:00, there were about twenty people walking around the living room and backyard. Bea had done a great job in planning the party, and she invited a bunch of people I didn't know because they didn't go to our school. My mom had been excited to help Bea decorate, and there were tables full of pizza, chips, and pretzels. There were lots of soda bottles with red cups stacked next to them. The lights had been dimmed, and the music was blasting. My mom and dad had gone out for a date night, and Henry was at a sleepover at his friend's house, so we had the house to ourselves.

I scanned the room for Jack and saw him standing by the table with the Bluetooth speaker, talking to Luke. Luke led me to think about Leanne, and Leanne made me think about Mark, so my mind looped again into a vicious cycle. I tried to distract myself and felt relieved when Grace walked into the party, but that feeling was only temporary. I remembered the conversation with Bea, and her words came hurtling at me like a hard boulder. I didn't mean to be a bad friend, but I was starting to grow feelings of suspicion against Grace. It wasn't like I wanted it to happen, but it just did, and I couldn't seem to turn those feelings off.

"Happy birthday, Bells," Grace said as she embraced me into a big, warm hug. I couldn't help but cringe when she called me Bells, and yet again I didn't have the heart to tell her to stop calling me by the nickname Leanne had given me.

"Thanks," I told her as I forced a smile. I wished I didn't have to force a smile when I was with her, as she was supposed to be one of my best friends.

"Do you mind if I just leave my bag here?" She pointed to an open spot against the wall.

"No, not at all," I said, and I knew I was staring at her bag. The thought that her notebook could be in there made me feel—I don't know—anxious, maybe. It was a strange feeling, one that I hadn't felt in a long time.

Grace could sense something was off with us, and I could too, but I wasn't sure whether it was my suspicion of her that was causing it, or some other problem in our friendship that hadn't been resolved from the beginning. "I'm going to go get a drink. Do you want anything?" she asked.

"No, I'm good."

"Shut up. You're the birthday girl. I'm getting you one," Grace said as she slipped into the crowd. I didn't argue, because I was distracted by how she left her bag next to me. Grace came back with two red cups in her hands and handed one to me. "Cheers," she said.

I took a sip. "Bleh, what is this?"

"It's just Coke."

"Is there something in it?"

Grace laughed, and I smiled at her the way that Bea would smile at her. My suspicions of Grace were starting to take over any and every time she did anything. There was something about Grace that was always over-the-top and theatrical—what if she would do something like we saw on TV, where she would give me a Coke that had something mixed into it? And I would get drunk without knowing and make a mess of everything? As much as I trusted Jack to make sure no one had brought any alcohol to the party, he was distracted now. I had never had alcohol before, and I didn't plan on it anytime soon.

Grace shrugged and sipped her drink. "Maybe it's one of those no-sugar, no-calorie types of Coke," she said. "Anyway, I'll see you around." She walked away without looking back. I sniffed my drink and didn't smell any alcohol in it. I put it down and looked for Grace again. If she was busy mingling at the party, it would give me the chance to do something much more important.

I went over to her bag slumped against the wall and grabbed her notebook. It was heavy and stuffed full of extra paper. I crossed my arms around it and ran upstairs without having enough time to think about or regret what I was doing.

I walked into my room and sat on my bed. I laid Grace's notebook down in front of me and paused before opening it. What was this mystery hovering around it? Did I even want to know? Maybe it was just a diary that she wrote in, and the entries would be boring, like a normal person's. But the more questions I asked, the less I believed that the answers I wanted were true. I needed to know what she was hiding. I opened the notebook.

Thirteen

I never understood how a person could be completely bad or evil. People could do bad things, but it didn't mean that they were necessarily evil. That was what made TV dramas exciting. It was just so far off from real life. In real life, someone didn't switch from being a good guy to a bad guy. But that was all about to change.

Sitting with Grace's notebook, I flipped through the pages, and at first, I could not believe my eyes. The pages were filled with pictures of Jack. There were detailed entries about everything Jack did, from what he had for lunch to how many points he'd scored during basketball practice. There were even strands of his hair taped to a page. It took me a minute to understand the date Grace had scribbled below the strands of hair. It was dated back to July of last summer, which was the summer before Grace moved here.

Somehow, she already knew Jack. Then it hit me—Grace was from Chicago, not Cleveland. When we left the ski lodge, Mark had called Jack the nickname he hated—Chicago. Jack must have spent some time in Chicago, where something happened that Mark knew about and hung over Jack's head. My mind raced—

Mark and Grace were old family friends. Did this mean that last summer, when Mark and Jack were still best friends, they went on a trip to Chicago and met with Grace? Did Grace follow Jack here?

The idea was crazy, but the notebook in front of me was *crazy*, and the whole thing made me feel sick. I thought about what Grace had said about disguises and costumes while we watched *Gossip Girl*. I remembered the afternoon at our room in the ski lodge when she had brought a suitcase stuffed with clothes and changed through five different outfits. She was able to make herself into a person I wanted to see. Then there were the glares I thought Bea shot at me, but they happened only when I was next to Grace.

Every time I had seen Grace scribbling, Jack was always nearby, and the night at the ski lodge, she must have recorded everything that happened at the hot tub with Jack. I remembered the way Mark mysteriously appeared early the next morning, as if he'd just happened to roll out of bed and found me sitting outside of our room door. Did that mean Mark was in on whatever plan Grace had hatched? It didn't hit me until I saw my name countless times on the pages dated before Grace and I were even friends that I understood how she had been watching me for a while. Even through everything I was learning, it did hurt to think that Grace was my friend only because I was dating Jack and she'd probably drop me as soon as I told him the truth.

"You know what they say about going through other people's belongings?" Grace asked, standing in the doorway. She kept her face downcast and in shadow, and even though we were in my room, I was scared by her staring at me from the corners of her eyes.

"Who are you? I mean, is your name even Grace?"

"It's Rachel. My middle name's Grace, but let's skip the chitchat, because you're going to help me get Jack."

"What the heck are you saying?" I said. "And what is this notebook? Don't you have a boyfriend back home?"

Grace laughed. I remembered now a few times when Grace would freeze up or get quiet around Jack and other times when she had tried to get his attention. During the ski trip, I had been so paranoid that Jack would get back with Leanne, when this whole time Grace was the one I should have been watching out for. "You made up your boyfriend, didn't you?" I said. "You've been in love with Jack this whole time? Why wouldn't Jack have said anything to me if you'd known each other before?"

"This may come as a shock to you," Grace said. "Jack and I fell in love last summer. That's right. L-O-V-E. Then the day before he was going back home to break up with Leanne, he fell off a jet ski and hit his head. When he woke up, he had no memory of his trip. He didn't tell you about any of this, I'm assuming."

"Well, how could he have, if he woke up with no memory?" I said. "But it doesn't matter, because I'm telling Jack about all of this now." I picked up the notebook from the bed and held it across my chest.

"Nuh-uh, I don't think so. Not unless you want me to tell Jack that you cheated on him and break his poor little heart."

"I was going to tell him anyway," I said, trying to stand my ground, even though it was more like standing my ground with wobbly legs.

"Fine, you want to play it that way. I'll tell everyone Bea's secret then, and she won't ever forgive you for selling her out, just because you wanted to tell Jack who I really am."

"So that's what you're holding over her?"

"And now I'm holding it over you too. You're going to listen to whatever I tell you to do—got it?"

I remembered the morning Bea and I talked in the bathroom. Bea was strong, but I knew that when she had told me the truth about her parents and who she really was, her face held a lot of pain. "Got it," I told Grace, reluctantly.

"Can't you at least try to pretend to be a little enthusiastic?" Grace said, yanking the notebook from my arms. "It's not that hard — to pretend, that is. I was your 'friend' for months, anyway."

"Got it," I said again with the most forced smile I could muster.

"Good." Her phone buzzed with a text, so she looked down at it, even though I could tell she didn't want to take her eyes off of me, not even for a second. "And now we're going downstairs."

Grace picked up her notebook from my bed and pushed my bedroom door wide open. She waited for me to walk down first. I tried to stall and hoped someone would come and save me, but Grace wasn't going to let that happen. "Come on, hurry up," she said, waving her phone at me, as though she could shoot me with it.

We slowly walked down the steps to where everyone was talking and dancing. I prayed that someone would save me once again, but, of course, no one else knew what was going on. I thought Grace was going to lead us outside to where Jack was, but when we got to the bottom of the stairs, Grace told me to stop, and she opened the front door. I hoped that was my chance to run away and find Bea so we could come up with a plan, but then I heard a voice that I dreaded. "Happy birthday, Leanne 2.0." I turned around to see the only person who could have possibly made my day any worse. "Surprise."

I looked at Mark. I had so many questions for him, but somehow the only word that could come out of my mouth was "Mark."

Bringing him to my party was a part of Grace's plan, and I fell right into it. Everything that had just happened between Grace and me was wiped from my mind as I focused on Mark. How could I ever explain to him that what he was doing, calling me Leanne 2.0, wasn't fair?

It wasn't fair that when he made out with Leanne, Jack found out right away, rather than having the secret burdening Leanne for weeks. It wasn't fair that Mark got a get-out-of-jail-free card and was able to run off to his family's ski lodge — that did actually exist despite everyone's doubts — but then chose to just show up here when he felt like it and remind me of what had happened between us. Most of all, it wasn't fair that when it came down to it, I knew, deep down, that to Jack, I was really nothing compared to Leanne. I knew Jack would fight a thousand — if not a million — times harder for her than for me, and as I looked at Mark, it was a truth that he seemed to know already.

"What? No 'Hey, Mark, how are you?' Or 'What's up?' Or 'What have you been up to?' Or even just 'Hi, Mark' would've been fine." He laughed.

"Please, stop talking," I said, looking over my shoulder, because as much as I hated it, I was afraid Jack was going to catch us — doing what? I wasn't sure, but I couldn't take any chances.

"Ouch."

"I'm gonna go talk to Jack," Grace said.

I had forgotten that Grace had been standing there. I wished I could also forget about the fact that I thought that our friendship had been real and genuine, so I made sure not to give her the satisfaction of turning around as she pranced away. I didn't want her to go to Jack, but something paralyzed me — fear, maybe? I tried to forget about Grace for the time being, because first I had to focus on getting rid of Mark. I glanced over my shoulder for a second to see Grace disappear into the crowd, and it seemed that everyone else was still enjoying the party and not really paying attention to Mark and me standing by the front door. I turned back to Mark. "I don't really care about your feelings right now," I said. "Jack's here, and everything's going to get a thousand times worse if he sees you talking to me, so please get out."

I feared I was being too transparent, but I didn't have time to be vague or to come up with complicated implications and wait for Mark to decipher them. I had to be straightforward and to the point so that he'd understand why he needed to leave.

"You didn't tell Jack? I'm not surprised," Mark said, stepping inside the house and closing the front door behind him.

I hated the way he could read people so well. I had to beat him at his own game, so with a straight face I said, "I could say the same thing about you."

"Ouch again," Mark said, as if he actually had feelings that I could hurt. "Why does everyone assume that I'm the villain in the story? Why can't you trust me?"

"Because you kissed your best friend's girlfriend—twice," I said, and my confidence broke down for a second as I flashed him a guilty smile.

"Okay, bad example." Mark shrugged off my last sentence. "Let's try something else . . . have I ever lied to you before? Be honest."

Mark smiled at his own question, which, despite myself, made me smile too. I wanted him to listen to me and be afraid to even be in my house with Jack around. I wanted to say something that would hit him hard, and I wanted to see the look on his face when I was able to come up with a time when he lied to me . . . except I couldn't. As hard as I tried, I came up blank, and I hated the smug smile he wore on his face as he watched me struggle. I didn't want to tell him that as much as I hated to admit it, he had never lied to me the way I knew Jack had, over and over again. Mark standing there made me uncomfortable, and in such an uncomfortable situation, I couldn't help but smile again. I shifted my body weight between my feet, back and forth, in an effort to stall.

"So?" Mark asked.

I hesitated as I went, for a last time, through all my memories of the conversations we'd had. "No," I said. "But the last time we talked, you were being vague and warning me about something or someone. What was I supposed to make of that?"

Then it hit me. I thought back to our strange encounter that early morning at the ski lodge. He had avoided my eyes and looked at the closed door of our room where Grace was sleeping. He knew Grace's plan — he had known all along and tried to warn me. The last thing he said was "I don't want to see you getting hurt too."

"Warned you? Warned you about who?" he asked. He was looking past my shoulder and surveying the room. I laughed about how this was as close to a lie as he'd come to telling me. I wished he'd cut the act and come clean already.

"Don't play dumb, Mark. I know."

He met my eyes again. "First of all, I don't play dumb. And, second, what do you know?"

"About Grace. That's what you were warning me about, right?"

"Yeah, yeah, and her whole thing with Jack," he said with a sigh of relief.

"Exactly," I said without even trying to conceal my excitement. There was finally someone who understood what was going on, someone I could trust.

"Wow, I'm just so relieved, you know?" Mark said, more relaxed than I'd ever seen him. It was like he had all of these guards up that I hadn't noticed until he had taken them all down.

Mark being more relaxed put me at ease too. "Okay, I trust you," I said. Even though it was scary to be vulnerable, it also felt good to stop whatever game we had been playing. Still, I had to ask, "You're not going to tell Jack about the kiss, are you?"

"No, because what you need to understand is that whatever happened between Leanne and me is very different from what happened between me and you."

"What are you talking about?"

"Later," he said, giving me a look that seemed to say he was sorry that he couldn't say more.

Just like that, he walked past me and disappeared into the crowd of people in the living room. Whatever happened to trust? I thought we could trust each other now that we both knew the truth about Grace . . . unless that wasn't the only secret he was hiding. I really hoped that wasn't the case, but I knew it was.

I surveyed the party. People were crowded in the dark living room and hanging out and dancing. Even though I didn't know everyone there, I knew who wasn't there—my parents, my old friends, Leanne. A part of me wished they were there to do something corny like stopping the music to bring out cake with bright candles. Then I pushed those feelings away and caught a glimpse of Jack. Even though he was standing just outside the sliding glass door, I could see how his eyes were lit up the way they used to be when he saw me—except now, he wasn't looking at me. He was looking at his stalker, who he was still clueless about.

Jack was smiling at Grace, who was animating her arms in the way people do only when they're talking about something they're really passionate about. Grace said something that made Jack laugh so hard that he clutched his stomach because it hurt to laugh. I couldn't think of a single time when I had made him laugh that hard. I was jealous even though I didn't want to be, and that feeling took me back to almost every interaction I'd ever witnessed between Jack and Leanne.

Watching Grace try to woo my boyfriend made me feel sick to my stomach. I didn't know what I should do—whether I should go outside and tell Jack everything, whether I should find Bea and ask her what we should do, or whether I should find Mark and tell him to leave. Instead, I turned around, opened the front door, and walked outside.

The night was quiet, other than the muted music playing in my house behind me. I was wearing high heels that Bea had let me borrow, and with a *click-clack*, *click-clack*, I walked down the path and to the sidewalk. I stared up at the stars in the sky, then back at my house. I tried to imagine seeing it the way other people saw it—the strangers who punched my address into their GPSs and rolled up in their cars for my party. There was the way Jack had seen it, the first time he'd walked me home and the many times after that. But there was also the way that my parents and Henry saw it. The way I saw it was different too, from how I saw it in the morning when I would just glance back at it as I left home for school. Right now, it was night, and I looked at it differently from how I had before, with the first party I'd ever thrown happening inside of it. There were people in almost every window.

"Bella?"

I turned around. Makenzie and Nicole walked toward me on the sidewalk. Makenzie had called out my name, and Nicole was behind her, unsure of what to say. Jade was still in the street, getting something out from the backseat of her car. I didn't know that Jade had passed her driver's license test or that her parents had gotten her a car. But I was sure there was a lot about all their lives that I had missed.

"Hey," I said, surprised. "What are you doing here?" They were dressed up, and Jade ran to catch up with Makenzie and

Nicole while holding a silver "Happy Birthday" balloon on a string.

"What a way to greet your friends," Makenzie said, rolling her eyes. "I told you we shouldn't have come," she said to Nicole and Jade.

"Bea invited us," Jade said, handing the balloon to me. "She said she invited everyone."

"Thanks," I said, taking the balloon. Then, because I couldn't help myself, I asked, "Did she invite Leanne too?" I wasn't even sure they would have the answer.

"Yeah, but Leanne didn't want to come," Nicole said quickly. She seemed really excited to be there, even though we hadn't talked since I lied to her about ditching Jade's birthday party. We stood there without saying anything, and her eyes drifted toward my house and to the party. "Should we go inside?" Nicole asked.

"Oh, yeah, of course," I said, "But—" I started, but stopped myself.

"What is it?" Makenzie asked, crossing her arms.

"It's just . . . I don't know if this is your scene."

Makenzie looked me up and down. "Why? Because you still think you're too good for us, ever since you started dating Jack? That your party is too cool now that a bunch of strangers are inside drinking and tearing up your house?"

With everything going on that night, especially with Grace and Mark, I exploded. "You assume that Jack's the bad guy. Jack doesn't drink, and he doesn't plan on it. If you took the time to get to know him like I have, you'd know that. But, no, you assume that he's some stupid jock who's going to ruin my life."

Makenzie snorted.

"Stop being so hard on her," Jade said in a soft voice to Makenzie. "She doesn't know."

"I don't know what?" I said. They must have thought they lost their friend to some stupid jock who was using her, but they didn't understand that Jack wasn't like that—he was so much more. He was my first love, and how could I explain that to Makenzie, who didn't want to think about love until she had a stable career, or Nicole, who'd never been in love despite talking about it way too much? Then there was Jade, who was in love but never talked about it. How could I know she felt the same way I did when she never shared how she felt? How could I ever explain to them how I felt about Jack when I knew they could never understand?

"Who do you think came up with the name 'sophomore slut'?" Makenzie asked.

I froze.

"It's true," Nicole said, stepping forward. "Leanne came to talk with us after the ski trip. She said she was worried that what was happening to you was exactly like what had happened to her."

"No." I shook my head. I remembered seeing Jack and Leanne talk quietly throughout the ski trip. They seemed as close as they were when they were dating. I was jealous, and deep in my heart, I knew that Jack cared more about Leanne than he did about me. After all, he'd told me, "I love you, D," without even realizing what he said. Maybe I really was just Leanne 2.0 to him.

I wasn't even sure why my old friends had bothered to come to my party. "What's between Jack and me is totally different from whatever was between Jack and Leanne," I said. "I know you think I'm in some bad relationship, but I'm not. Next time you try to show up at my house and judge my life, don't do it based on rumors or assumptions you have. When you get facts, then you can come to me, but the only truth you'll find is that I'm in love." It all sounded forced. I hoped they didn't realize that I said all that to myself more than to them.

"Jack cheated on Leanne first!" Nicole said.

A muted crash, followed by laughter, drifted from my house. I turned to stare at the door, but I didn't care what was happening inside. Then, to test out my theory, I said slowly, "Last summer. In Chicago. With Grace."

"Yeah," Nicole said, staring at me, surprised, along with Makenzie and Jade.

"How did you know?" Makenzie asked.

I put my face in my hands and dropped the balloon string. The balloon floated away from us and into the night sky. I wished I was wrong, but my old friends just showed up out of nowhere like a trio of witches and confirmed that my crazy theory was right.

"Hey," Jade said, coming over to me and putting her hand on my back. "You know how Nicole and Makenzie can be. We're just worried about you, and Leanne told us her side of the story, because she didn't think she could get to you another way."

"Okay," I said, looking at Jade again. "Tell me the rest of it."

Nicole cut in. "The short of it is that on a random trip to Chicago, Jack kissed Grace. He probably thought he'd never see her again, even though Grace and Mark were close, and he didn't know that Grace was about to move to our school. So afterward, Grace got crazy jealous and wanted to break him and Leanne up. She made up some plan for Mark to make it look like something was happening with Leanne in Jack's room."

It was then I realized that Nicole was enjoying all this, that she finally had a reason to be involved in our lives. Why couldn't Leanne have been the person to show up unannounced at my party and tell me her side of the story herself? But her thinking had been right—I wouldn't have believed her. I wouldn't have listened to her. I took a breath.

"And then Jack started telling everyone that Leanne cheated on him and started calling her the sophomore slut?" I asked.

I remembered the Monday after Jack's mom's wedding, when no one at school would be friends with Leanne anymore. She had gone from being the most popular girl in our grade to a total outcast. "How did he come up with that name?" I asked. "And why didn't Leanne tell us sooner?"

"She tried, but no one would believe her," Makenzie said.

That sick feeling returned to my stomach again. My mouth filled with saliva and the taste of the weird Coke. I wanted to throw up. I wanted to tell Makenzie, Nicole, and Jade that they were lying. I wanted to say they were jealous of me and trying to ruin my birthday party. But I knew all of that was untrue. "I can't deal with any of this right now," I said. "I'm going back inside."

"Let's go," Makenzie said.

Nicole started to follow me into the house.

"No, dummy. We're going home," Makenzie said.

"What? We're not going in?" Nicole asked.

"No," Makenzie said, eyeing my house. "Some friends you have in there."

Jade stood still, before catching up with me to give me a hug. "Bye, Bella," she said. "Check back in with me tomorrow or Monday. I'm always here for you." Then she ran to unlock her car that beeped twice as they all got inside.

From my doorstep, I watched my old friends drive away. The feeling of needing to throw up right then and there passed, but with everything that happened that night, I was done partying. I opened the door to go inside, and a few people turned to stare at me. I wondered whether anyone even noticed that I was gone. I started to walk up the stairs. I wanted to get into bed to process everything that had happened, but as I got to the middle of the staircase, I heard Mark's voice again. "Hey, Bella, where are you going?"

I turned around to see him at the foot of the stairs. Maybe he was trying to rescue me, but then again, how could he have known what I was feeling? "What do you want?" I asked harshly, because if he really did what my old friends said, I didn't owe him anything.

He cocked his head sideways, signaling for me to come back downstairs. I walked back down even though I knew I would probably regret it.

"You look like you could use a friend right about now," Mark said.

"And that friend is you?" I asked. "I need to be alone. I was just going to bed."

"This is your party. You can do whatever you want."

"Yeah, okay, see you."

"Hey, wait up," Mark touched my arm. "Listen, before you go, I just wanted to say that I'm here for you, and I won't run off again like I did earlier."

"Bad habit?" I said, referring to how he'd run off at the ski lodge too.

"You have no idea."

"Thank you, that was sweet."

"And one more thing."

"What's that?"

"I do trust you, and I care about what you think of me."

"Thanks." I wasn't sure anymore whether this was a continuation of some game. Maybe he was still loyal to Grace, and after I told him I'd figured her out, they came up with another plan. Then, in thinking about Grace, I had to ask another question. I looked into Mark's green eyes and asked, "What could have happened to Grace to make her so crazy about Jack?"

Mark's face froze.

"What about Jack?" Jack asked. He had come up beside us, with Grace standing close by.

"Hey, Chicago, what's up?" Mark asked.

"You're at my girlfriend's party—you wanna tell me what's up?"

"Chill," Mark said, looking around them. Luke stopped the music at the other side of the room, and everyone at the party turned to stare at Mark and Jack standing at the foot of the stairs. "I just got back into town. My parents didn't really like the 'mountain hippie school' I was going to, so I'm staying at my cousin's—the one who lives right outside of town, remember?"

"That's not what I asked you. What are you doing at Bella's house, talking to her like you want to go upstairs?"

The room gasped. Even though I'd learned vile secrets about the two of them, there was still a part of me that liked the feeling of being wanted by them both. It felt really good. But I had to intervene, so I told Jack, "Don't be paranoid. Mark was just leaving."

Mark flashed me an apologetic look, too quick for Jack to see and almost too quick for me to have even noticed, but I caught it. I wasn't really sure what he was going to do. Instead, Mark put his hands up and said, "Okay, fine, I'm not here to bother you." He walked over to the door and grabbed the handle. "You're exactly the same, Chicago—"

From the corner of my eye, I could see Grace tense up with a smile frozen onto her face.

"What did I say about you calling me that?" Jack said, and before anyone could stop him, he stepped forward and punched Mark so hard in the face that the side of Mark's head bounced against the door.

I screamed. Mark clutched his right cheek. He didn't make a move to hit Jack. I stared at them, horrified, then turned to see Jack return to my side and wrap his arm around my waist. Everyone's eyes were locked on Jack and me, Jack's girlfriend.

Grace's face stayed frozen, but her eyes were cold and jealous. I wriggled out of Jack's arms. "Who are you trying to impress by being pissed off?" I shouted.

And just like that, he took his arm off of me and yelled, "Screw you! I'm done!" as he made his way through the crowded living room and out of the sliding glass door. Everyone else was silent and watched him go. I wasn't sure whether he had said that to me, or to Mark, or to everyone watching. Maybe Jack was so mad that it didn't matter.

As he left, I saw my parents' car headlights beam against the grass. The room was so quiet that we could hear the music from their car, my dad's cheerful voice, and my mom's high heels clacking against the driveway. "Well, my parents are back," I told everyone without trying to hide the half-heartedness in my voice. "Party's over. Thanks for coming." I turned around and went upstairs before anyone could say anything more.

Alone in my room, I checked my watch, which I almost forgot I was still wearing, and saw that it was 12:02 a.m. It was officially my sixteenth birthday. In some other parallel universe, where nothing about the night happened and I still thought Jack was a good guy, he was supposed to have some big surprise for me at midnight.

While still wearing my dress and jewelry, I crawled into bed. My phone beeped with a text, and the same childish part of me hoped that it was Jack saying that the whole night had all been a big joke—everything from Grace's notebook, to the real story of what happened with Leanne, to the fight between him and Mark. He could say that it was all a big dramatic prank and that my birthday present was waiting outside, even though it was five minutes later than he'd promised. Maybe with a text like that, we could forget everything that had happened and go back to the way things were, when we were still living inside a fantasy and everything was fine.

Instead, I saw that it was a text from a blocked number that said: *Good job tonight. It's like you're doing my work for me. Just keep doing what you're doing and be distant and whatever. You'll hear from me soon.* Although it was way too dramatic, I wasn't surprised because Grace — Rachel, or whatever her name was — was dramatic by definition.

I could hear voices from downstairs. Bea was talking to my mom. I knew I should go downstairs and at least offer to help them clean up. Maybe we could even have some cake like I'd wanted. I felt too bad, though, and snuggled deeper inside my bed. My hand hit the gift bag that Jack had given me in the beginning of the evening. I dug the gift bag out from the blankets and reached into it to take out the gift card inside. Then I laughed when I saw the expiration date. It was like the universe was playing some twisted joke on me. The expiration date was 9/29/18, which just happened to be the day of Jack's mom's wedding — the day that Jack and Leanne broke up. That's when the twisted part of the joke caught up to me and I stopped laughing. How had Jack ever been the good guy in my story?

Fourteen

An hour later, I was still awake. Bea had come upstairs to check on me after helping my mom clean up most of the trash. "I know parties were never your thing," she said when she found me with my eyes puffy and red. She sat by my side and listened as I told her everything. Bea had somehow missed most of the drama. She'd had some unwanted encounter with Grace in the bathroom, where Grace yelled at her for letting me find out about her real identity. When I heard that last part, I wished I could be the one to comfort Bea, or to at least apologize, because it was bad to be on Grace's bad side. I could say that now from experience, but I'd been on Grace's bad side for only one night, and I really had no idea how long Bea had been on it.

"Do you really have to put up with Grace?" I asked. "Do you have to hide who you are?"

Even though having a house party full of strangers wasn't that fun for me, it was something that was still important to Bea. "I can't risk it," she said, shaking her head. "I can't let go of that part of myself. Not yet at least."

I looked over at the clock on my nightstand to see that it was already 1:15 a.m. I looked over at Bea, and a pang of regret hit me. Why was I making her stay with me when her life and her situation were much worse than my own?

"You can go home, you know," I said with my voice way hoarser than I expected.

"Oh, I know," she replied. Her smile was tired. I remembered how at her own sleepover, she'd had such high energy until 4:00 in the morning—which made me think about all that time I had just seen Bea's front, rather than the real her. I had to know the real story. I had to ask her. "Hey, so what I just told you—is it true? Were you in on it?"

Bea paused. "I don't know all the details . . ." she began.

"But it *is* true," I said, finishing her sentence.

She nodded. "Mostly . . . although, I haven't exactly thought about what happened in the way you just put it."

"You mean Leanne's side of the story?" I asked. "Even though you knew what happened this whole time. You were in on it. Keeping Jack's secret. Helping Grace. Spreading rumors about Leanne."

Bea got up to leave. "I'm not proud of helping her, Bella, but you making me feel like the villain isn't going to help anyone. We've all done things we're not proud of. We can feel bad about them and want to do better, but we can make real change only a little bit at a time."

For the rest of the weekend, I managed to distract myself with homework. I knew come Monday, I'd have to face Jack, Mark, Grace, and Bea at school. I wasn't really sure how I was going to do that. I also had to face Leanne, but I didn't know yet what I should say.

It was also possible that the "real story" of what happened at Jack's mom's wedding wasn't either Leanne's story or Jack's story. At first, I had trouble sitting with the idea that Leanne had gone to our old friends to tell them what had happened. Maybe she really just wanted to break Jack and me up. But that sounded manipulative, like Grace, and not something Leanne would do.

Then I had trouble thinking about how Jack was the one who had cheated on Leanne. How could Jack do something like that and be so heartless? And how could he hit his head right after it happened, get amnesia, and forget the whole thing? I had even more trouble with the idea that he was the one who came up with the nickname for Leanne. I'd spent a lot of time getting to know him, and even though he had trouble controlling his anger sometimes, there was a part of him that was thoughtful, sweet, and kind. He wrote love poems for fun, after all. I had to figure out the real story for myself. Especially when I knew Jack loved Leanne. It just didn't make sense that he would cheat on her and lie about it. If he loved Leanne, how could he hurt her?

On Monday morning, I considered pretending I was sick so I could stay at home. I did have a stomachache all weekend. But then I thought, what would people at school think if I didn't show up after all the drama that happened at my party? There was no doubt in my mind that the kids in my grade, and maybe even the whole school, were making up countless rumors about what had happened over the weekend.

I spent way too long staring at my closet trying to decide what to wear. It was stupid and silly. Why was I dressing to impress anyone? I didn't know how to answer that question, but I finally picked out an olive-green sweater and jeans. I'd always thought that green was an ugly color, but Bea had picked it out from my closet last weekend and said that olive green suited me. She said it was my color, and I put it on to see that she had been right. I hoped she wasn't still mad. I tied my hair into a high ponytail and put on a bracelet Bea had left behind from our party prep. I looked in the mirror when I was done getting ready, and even though my outfit and hair looked nice, I couldn't help but think it didn't matter with my expression full of dread.

When I got to school, I ignored all of the eyes on me and the whispering I knew was going on behind my back. I kept my head down, even though I knew staying quiet wouldn't make the rumors disappear. I stared at the ground as I passed Makenzie's locker, where she, Nicole, and Jade were clustered together. From the corner of my eye, I could see Jade move to say hi to me, but I turned my face away before she had a chance to catch my attention.

I had thought a lot about the way they'd shown up at my house over the weekend, and even though they may have thought they were doing the right thing, I realized that, with Nicole and Makenzie anyway, we were never real friends from the beginning. They both thought they were being real friends, but they didn't actually care about Leanne or me or how we were feeling. Jade may have cared, but she always went along with the two of them, as though she couldn't manage to say or do anything by herself. I couldn't honestly imagine being friends with them again. I had changed so much in the past few months. I couldn't go back, and I didn't think I wanted to.

If I was a different type of person, maybe it would have been good to have my old friends back on my side. Maybe I was wrong to stay quiet, because it would show everyone else that I had given up. Maybe people were already starting to call me the new sophomore slut. But even if they were, maybe I should have been strong enough to keep my head up, because then I would have seen Jack waiting for me by my locker. I didn't see him until it was too late to ignore him or hide. Seeing him stand there, stiff and angry, sent a shiver down my spine.

"You're unbelievable, Bella—do you know that?" Jack said with a booming voice that attracted a lot of attention.

I opened my mouth to answer him, even though I wasn't exactly sure what to say. He waved for me to follow him through a set of double doors and out of the hallway so we could be out of earshot from the onlookers he was definitely aware of.

"You've heard all the rumors, haven't you?" he asked, once we were outside. "People are saying that you cheated on me with Mark at your party. They're saying you're like a second Leanne or something, you know that?"

"Nothing happened with Mark and me at my party," I said, weakly. "Who told you that?"

Jack ignored what I said and continued ranting. "I said I loved you. No one can love you if you don't love yourself."

His last sentence struck me. Even in the mess we were in, he was able to say something clear and true. "I do love myself," I stammered. "And I love you."

"Yeah, sure you do," Jack said. "When we first met, I said I'd never make you feel like you were unwanted. I took you out and invited you to my games and introduced you to all my friends. You were the one who distanced yourself from me, and now there's this rumor about you and Mark. I can't handle this right now, Bella, and now Mark's back. Why didn't you think to tell me the second you saw him walk through the door? Do you have any idea what he's done to me? You can't hurt me like Leanne did—you can't, okay?"

I almost forgot that he didn't know that whatever happened between Leanne and Mark was a setup. I wanted to tell him the truth — Leanne never cheated on him — and watch his eyes light up the way they used to. But then he wouldn't look at me that way; he'd look at her. Was it selfish that I wanted Jack to myself?

After asking so many questions without expecting an answer, I realized strangely that Jack might have been talking to himself more than to me, because before I knew it, he was shaking and his eyes were glassy. He wrapped his arms around me and drew me into a hug. He cried into my shoulder. Maybe he wanted me to feel sorry for him, but it was then I realized that whatever coldness and selfishness had formed in his heart were still there. Jack said I needed to love myself first, but maybe he was really talking to himself. He could not see past his own pain enough to see anything, or anyone, else. Was it really worth having him if he couldn't see me?

"I'm unbelievable, Jack?" I said, pulling away. "Tell me the truth. Did you know Grace before she moved here?"

He didn't answer for a moment as he tried to find an excuse. "I could tell you the truth, but it's not like you're going to believe me."

I was about to explode and tell him about Grace's stalker journal, but even though Bea and I had fought after my party, I still couldn't betray her, so instead I said, "Grace says you two fell in love last summer and then you fell off a jet ski and lost your memory."

Jack laughed. "Yeah, we met last summer, but we definitely didn't fall in love. I hardly know who she is."

"Why didn't you say anything? About going to Chicago? About falling off a jet ski?"

"Look, that was from a time when Mark and I were still friends, and it's not something I want to think about."

I wanted to argue, but before he gave me the chance, he turned the questioning around to me. "How about you tell me the truth first?" he said. "Did anything happen between you and Mark?"

This was the moment everything was going to fall apart. We both knew it somewhere in our hearts. I avoided his eyes, and in a quiet voice, I said, "Mark kissed me at the ski lodge." I wanted to put up more of a fight, but what was the use? I was starting to wonder whether Jack was even worth all of the trouble.

"At the ski lodge?" Jack yelled. "You kept that from me all this time? You could have done this to me with anyone, but you chose *him*, of all people? How could you do this to me? I told you I loved you. I did everything right, and this—*this*—is how you repay me?"

I shot a look back at Jack. "Now it's your turn. Did you know Grace before she moved here? Because she's gone insane over you. And how was Leanne the one who became the social outcast from all of this?"

He ignored my question. "You're unbelievable. I gave you everything."

"You're the unbelievable one," I said. "Why are you avoiding my questions? Because you're afraid of telling me the truth?"

"Why does Grace matter?" Jack said. "What happened between us was forever ago. You and I, we're happening right now."

So there was at least some truth to Grace's story. It was then I knew that Jack and I were breaking up. I wondered whether us breaking up meant giving up every moment we'd had together and saying that it didn't mean anything. I wondered whether it meant that our first conversation wasn't as genuine as I'd thought it was or whether it meant every trip to Tony's didn't mean anything. I wondered whether it meant every time he'd said the word "love," it was never directed at me.

The morning light was just starting to become strong, and for some reason, I became aware of our shadows facing each other against the wall. Even though I was finally starting to see the real Jack, and maybe he was just starting to see the real me, it was still painful for me to realize what was happening. I let the tears fall down my face. "Then just tell me this," I said. "During the ski trip, did you want to get back together with Leanne?"

He looked at me with those clear blue eyes I'd fallen in love with that were about to shatter my heart. "First, you're obsessed with Leanne, and then Grace, and then back to Leanne," he said. Then he turned his gaze away from me, and it seemed like an idea crossed his mind. "I should've never let you sit down next to me," he said. "I only did it 'cause you reminded me of Leanne and I loved her and not you. I never loved you, Bella. You are one of the most annoying, irritating, infuriating, and exasperating people I know. I don't know how I put up with you for so long, and honestly, I don't know how anyone could. I mean, you really think *he* can love you? He's one of the most selfish people I know. He's only hanging out with you to make me jealous, you know. It's not like he has any actual feelings for you . . . and of course you were stupid enough to believe that he did."

Jack shouldn't have said any of that to me, and I knew that he knew that. There had to be a reason behind it all—there just had to.

"I don't understand," I told him softly as I tried to hide the tears brewing in my eyes. But what was the point?

"Do I have to spell it out for you? God, you're so stupid."

I had to fight back; I had to say something. I opened my mouth, but no words would come out. In truth, I didn't really know what I was going to say. All I knew was that I shouldn't have to say anything because I shouldn't even be in this position. I wasn't stupid, like he said I was. I just didn't want what was about to happen next to happen. He was breaking up with me, and the next step was to *spell it out* for me. The breakup was what I wanted, I thought. The way he did it, though, not so much. Maybe I couldn't find any words because he wasn't supposed to break up with me this way. He wasn't supposed to pick at every insecurity and take my vulnerabilities only to use them against me. Jack wasn't supposed to do all of this to me. He was supposed to love me, and that's why I found myself speechless.

"I. Am. Breaking. Up. With. You," he said in the most condescending tone possible. It was like he was trying to make me hate him.

My lip started quivering again, and that's when I saw the look on his face like he had just won or something. Everyone had been right all along: I had just been some sick game to him. The objective was to take all the feelings I had and destroy them in every possible way. I made sure to look at him with as much hate and anger as I could muster because I wanted him to remember me that way. In that moment, I knew I'd never look at him lovingly ever again, and most of all, I'd never love him ever again. That was when the scary part hit me: what if I'd never love again?

"It's been over between us for a while, hasn't it?" I asked.

"Yup," he said.

He didn't have to say anything for me to know the truth. This is what should've been best, but there was just something I couldn't let go.

I left Jack there and pushed back open the double doors to go to class. It hurt that we were breaking up, and it hurt even more that he didn't chase after me to apologize, or to say that we could try again, or to say that everything we'd just told each other wasn't actually true.

I went into the girls' bathroom and sobbed. I wished that Bea would just happen to walk in again, like she had the time I'd come in after the meeting with the principal and my parents. But Bea didn't come, and even with my life falling apart, there was no way I could be late for class, so I washed my face and put on a pair of sunglasses to hide my puffy eyes, only to have the bell ring the second I opened the bathroom door.

When I walked into class, Mark was there. I didn't know why that caught me so off guard. I knew Mark had transferred back, but I didn't think it would happen so fast, and I definitely didn't expect him to be in my class, sitting in the seat next to mine. I was late, and the teacher had already begun the lesson, which meant I couldn't switch seats, especially since the only available seat was mine. Mark noticed what was going on and smiled mischievously as I sat down. "Mark," I said. I didn't know what else to say. I didn't think there were words I could use to describe how I was feeling.

"That's the same greeting I got Friday night, Leanne 2.0," Mark whispered.

"Bella," I said, annoyed. The whole Leanne 2.0 thing started to spook me, and I needed to push it out of my head if I wanted to survive the week, or even the day.

"Is this what you're doing now, just saying people's names? Wouldn't you prefer sentences?"

"What?" I asked him, only now becoming aware I had been stuck in my thoughts. I didn't want to explain that to Mark. I didn't owe him any explanations, so I opened my notebook and tried to look busy and doodled a stick figure with sunglasses while trying to calm my nerves "Whatcha drawing there?" Mark said, leaning over.

"Why can't you leave me alone?" I asked.

There were voices behind us, whispering so loud that it was obvious I was meant to hear what they were saying. "Bella just pounced on the opportunity to get a boyfriend because she wouldn't have gotten one otherwise; she's just so desperate," one voice said.

"Look, she's already sitting up there, next to the new guy. She can't wait to move on to her next crush," another voice said.

Mark turned around. "Hey, my name's Mark, and I'm not the new guy," he said. "And if you have something to say about Bella, ask her to turn around and look her in the eye as you say it to her."

I shot a glance at the teacher to see whether he'd tell all of us to be quiet, but he was distracted at his desk shuffling through papers. The voices were quiet. One of them mumbled, "Sorry." I stayed hunched over my desk but met Mark's gaze as he turned around again. He winked.

"I don't need rescuing, Mark," I said.

"Sure you don't, Leanne 2.0," he said.

"Will you stop calling me that?" I asked. I wasn't sure whether my voice was shaking from how I'd just sobbed a few minutes earlier, but I continued. "Anyway, if you haven't noticed, Leanne is actually in this class—sitting in the back row, you'll be happy to know."

"What's that supposed to mean?"

"I'm not stupid, Mark. I know what guys like you do."

"Guys like me?" He asked, amused.

"Yeah, you kiss someone and ruin their life, only to forget about them."

That only seemed to make him smile. "Okay, I thought you picked up on it during our last conversation. You know that whole thing that happened with Leanne and me was different from the thing that happened between you and me, but clearly, you're not as smart as I gave you credit for, so to set the record straight, I never kissed Leanne."

"You didn't?" I knew Mark and Grace had some plan to make it seem like Mark and Leanne were doing something in Jack's room, but it never occurred to me that Mark didn't do anything so much as kiss her.

"No, I didn't. Now will you stop being mad at me?

I wanted to say yes. I wanted to say yes so badly, but I couldn't. Something was still wrong. I looked back to glance at Leanne, who for a second glanced at me before turning her attention forward again.

"Why did you go along with Grace's plan? Why did you have to make life so hard for Leanne?" I asked Mark.

"I don't know. I guess I just . . . I don't know."

"That's just it. You, Jack, Grace—or whatever the hell her name is—you're all the same. You like to play people, and until you figure yourself out, you'll just move on to the next person and won't ever stop."

Mark shrugged. "Yeah, whatever. I'll stop calling you Leanne 2.0. You'll never be as hot as her anyway."

I looked at him in disbelief. I had been willing to jeopardize my relationship with Jack over kissing him. A part of me had liked him—whether it was the cold green eyes or the way he just seemed to read people, I wasn't sure. I watched as what Mark had just said registered on his face.

"Shoot, Bella, I'm sorry. It wasn't supposed to come out like that." I didn't believe him. The way he said my name sent chills down my spine just like when he called me Leanne 2.0. Everything about Mark had made me uncomfortable from the moment he measured my feet at the ski lodge, and I should've taken that as a sign much sooner.

"No, Mark, I'm sorry." And right on cue the bell rang, so I walked out and didn't look back.

That afternoon, I found myself sitting at my desk at home, staring out the window. I was supposed to be doing my homework and working hard in school and all, but somehow I had ended up sitting at my desk for two hours doing nothing. It wasn't even like I was binging a show on Netflix and lost track of time; I really was sitting at my desk while hours escaped me. I thought about things and somehow ended up getting caught in a never-ending black hole of thoughts.

I took my laptop out from my backpack and opened a blank document. I never thought I'd come back to writing just because I felt like it, especially because it was something that Jack had both introduced me to and destroyed my interest in. But I was curious—could I point to the exact moment when our relationship started to go downhill? Was it right after Jack told me "I love you"? I had felt the happiest I ever was that night. Why couldn't we have just stayed in that feeling forever? I started typing:

Maybe I want to feel loved, but why does that feel so wrong?

It's crazy because all the ways that my life seemed to fall apart seemed to come from how I just wanted someone to love. It sounds so stupid to say it now, with everything that happened, and there's still that part of me that wants to forget everything and go back to Jack without seeming naive or innocent.

If in every book and movie the sixteen-year-old girl falls in love, why was it so wrong for me to want that for myself? I just wanted to be one of those girls in those romantic high school movies who falls in love . . . but it was such a mess. What if this need to feel love was also a part of Grace's insane reasoning for stalking Jack? Maybe it's actually the same as my reasoning too, of wanting to fall in love with Jack—only how it played out in real life was very different.

The first time we went to the writing club, the broad topic we had to write about was "The Universe." Jack wrote about being trapped. I wrote about being trapped. That's how it all started, with this feeling of being trapped. I didn't like who I was before I met Jack, and I didn't like the way I seemed trapped with the same three friends. What if my being with Jack was just some way to escape that? What if we were just each other's ways of escaping something?

It's funny actually, in that ironic kind of way, that the newfound freedom I'd felt only led to me feeling even more trapped.

I've felt trapped in every single friendship or relationship I've made since then, and I don't want to feel that way anymore. Maybe, despite how much I wanted it, maybe I wasn't ready to fall in love and be with Jack. That's so hard for me to admit, but now that I write it down, I can see how there's some truth to it.

I looked at my entry and felt better after writing down what I was thinking, but I still didn't feel happy. I wondered whether seeing things honestly wasn't actually better than staying clueless in the fantasy. Who cares if, at the end, we were happy?

Early the next morning, I woke up to my phone buzzing on my nightstand. I wished I could stay in my dreams forever. I wished I could forget my life. Still, I picked up my phone and in a sleepy voice said, "Hey."

"Look out your window," Jack said.

"Jack?" I sat up, much more awake.

"Just look out your window. I have a surprise."

As I got out of bed, the sunlight was bright and strong, even though it was only 6:00 a.m. I looked out at the display of roses strewn across my driveway that must have taken him all night to set up. They spelled out a poem:

These roses may be red,
but I can tell you're blue.
I'd like to leave nothing unsaid,
And tell you I love you.
I'm sorry for ruining your surprise,
Which hopefully won't lead to our relationship's demise.
I'd like for you to give me a second chance,
We're going on a trip, and no you won't have to dance.
Come downstairs or else . . .

This was one of the sweetest things he'd ever done, if not *the* sweetest. I had to laugh at the last line, which seemed so out of place but just managed to work. Either way, I rushed downstairs and opened the front door to see Jack with two tickets in his hand—they were day passes to Thrillpark! It was the one amusement park that was less than a two-hour drive from our small town. Thrillpark was notorious for being overpriced, which was why most people from town avoided it, but Jack was willing to pay for me. My face must have given me away because Jack grinned and said, "You're welcome."

I hugged him in response and couldn't remember the last time I had hugged him and felt secure in his arms. I could feel his body warmth through his jacket he insisted on wearing, even though spring came really early this year.

But there was school. It wasn't like I could just miss a random school day to go to an amusement park. "Jack, we can't do this," I said.

"Why not? I've gotten everything taken care of and thought out to the very last detail. You're not getting out of this, Carter."

"Carter? You've never called me that."

"I don't know—I just wanted to try it, I guess." He shrugged.

"Anyway, Jack, we can't ditch school."

"Ooh, I knew you were gonna say that one, but I didn't think it would be the first. So here's what you'll do. You'll call twice as both our moms."

"Uh, shouldn't you also call as my dad or something? Won't the office lady recognize my voice if I call her twice?"

"Like I said, it's all thought out. It's for a good reason. As you know, the office lady has it out for me and is also hardcore crushing on me. I bet she has some creepy notebook where she writes stuff about me and collects hair samples or something. I mean how busy can an office lady actually be? Anyway, she would recognize my voice from miles away, so it will just be better if you call twice."

I could tell he was trying to make a joke, and it would have been so funny if he didn't just describe Grace. That sent a cold shiver down my spine. I knew Grace would hate this—the whole amusement park date that Jack had planned out so perfectly. It would annoy Grace so much if I went on this date with Jack, so I decided to say yes.

"Okay, sounds like a plan," I said.

"Really? That's it? No more questions?" he asked, more shocked than I expected him to be.

"No more questions."

"Okay, then. I thought this part would take a lot longer, but I guess we can get going."

"I need to change," I said, as I watched his eyes scan my pajamas.

"Nah, you're fine," he said.

I thought about how I never really wanted to care about what I was wearing, so I smiled and said, "Great! I love it, okay," and followed Jack out to his car while wearing my pajamas, which were really just a T-shirt and sweatpants. When we got into Jack's car, he put on sunglasses and said, "So the thing is I don't actually have my driver's license."

"Why didn't you tell me earlier?" I asked. I should have been worried, but the more I thought about our trip to Thrillpark, the more I wanted to go.

"I didn't want to give you a reason not to go."

"Thanks," I said simply.

"For what?"

"For being honest. For all of this. For everything, really."

"You don't have to thank me," Jack said, cranking up the volume on his stereo.

We had a blast during the car ride, and I wouldn't have had it any other way. We laughed, we joked, and we fought, only to forgive each other within seconds. We talked, looked at the ever-changing views outside of the car windows, and talked about that too. Talking with Jack had never been easier, which made me wonder how I had been so wrong before about everything between us falling apart.

When we got to Thrillpark, we were the only people there, because it was early in the morning on a school day. This meant there were no lines. We gave each other a high five and ran into the park. The first roller coaster we went to was the Thriller. It had two huge loops that made us feel like we were going to fall out of the seat and splat onto the ground. Then we headed to Fall Rider. When the ride took a sharp turn and I leaned into Jack, he didn't stiffen or shift away, and neither did I. After weeks, we finally felt comfortable with each other again, and it felt really good.

After that, Jack helped me out of the ride, took my hand, and ran with me for no apparent reason to the next ride, the Snow-flake, which was an indoor ride with a snow machine. Instead of blowing out snow, the machine spat out water, and we got soaked. As soon as we got splashed, I turned to Jack, hoping he wouldn't be angry, because of all days, that was the day I couldn't handle him being angry when we were deserted together at Thrillpark.

To my surprise, he let out a laugh, and I let myself laugh too. We couldn't stop ourselves, and we laughed and laughed to the point where we were nearly crying and our stomachs hurt so much that we could hardly breathe.

We walked out of the ride together and walked into the gift shop that sold towels next to the Snowflake. We were about to buy them, but when we saw the price hanging above the bin, Jack decided to shove them under his shirt. The funniest part was that the cashier barely noticed us, and when she did look up to see Jack with the towels already stuffed inside his shirt, Jack gave her some sort of stare that either scared her or confused her, but it was enough for her to focus her attention back to whatever tabloid magazine she was flipping through.

As soon as we got outside, Jack pulled out the towels from underneath his shirt, and I didn't even care that they were wet from him. I wrapped one around myself and realized then how cold I'd been before. Jack noticed my shivering and put his arm around my shoulder. I couldn't remember the last time I'd been so happy by Jack's side, but there I was, with a huge smile on my face from his sweet gesture.

We walked over to the lunch place, where the only menu option was the Yummy Thrillmeal Packs. The meals were expensive, but it was okay, because Jack saved enough from not buying the towels. The Yummy Thrillmeal Pack consisted of hard, over-cooked pasta with drippy tomato sauce that got everywhere, a sour-salty-tasting water bottle, and a bag of potato chips that appeared to be full but had only five chips in it.

We sat down at a picnic table in the Thrillpark Eating Area and opened up the Yummy Thrillmeal Packs. Jack took a forkful of pasta and started chewing on it like a donkey, and I couldn't help laughing, so he continued the act, making more obnoxious chews with louder noises. When he was done, he opened up his sour-salty water bottle, but that was just as I attempted to eat the pasta. I, of course, had to beat Jack in the unspoken contest of who could eat more like a donkey, so I took it as a sign that I'd won when Jack spit out his sour-salty water as he laughed.

When I had decided that I won the contest, Jack wasn't very happy with me, so he opened his bag of chips, took out a handful, and threw them at me. There'd been only five chips inside the bag, which meant that he'd thrown all of them at me. I opened my bag and threw all of my potato chips at him. We picked up the chips from the ground and threw them at each other again until they crumbled into dust and we were on the floor, side by side, laughing at how much fun we were having.

Just like all days, good days had to come to an end too. We walked slowly to the Thrillparking Lot and were surprised by how much we didn't want to leave. I put my hand in Jack's as we walked toward his car. I looked over at Jack to see him yawn, and I smiled because he had just given me the chance to start yet another conversation with him. "What, am I really boring?" I asked.

"Ha ha, very funny. I'm just tired, and no one drinks the coffee here unless they want a heart attack, but other than that I'm fine."

"You sure you'll be okay driving?"

"Yeah, I told you I'm fine. Now I have a very important question to ask you."

"Which is?"

"Did *you* have fun today?"

"Yes, I did. I can't even begin to tell you how grateful I am."

He leaned in and kissed me as a "you're welcome." I couldn't remember the last time we had kissed. What if every day with Jack could be like this? We had fun in the way I hadn't had fun in a long time.

We got into his car, and maybe it was just the sun, but for the first time in a while, I saw Jack's eyes light up, just like the way they used to in the beginning when he'd talk to me and I felt I was floating on a cloud. I rested my hand on the center console between us, and Jack took my hand in his as he pulled out of the Thrillparking lot. I was falling in love with him all over again. I couldn't have felt safer with him by my side.

I watched Jack drive. I could tell he liked the feeling of being in control, cruising down a road. I could tell driving made him feel free, even if he didn't say it. I saw the way he smiled when he rolled down the windows and let the wind blow in his face. It wasn't just that: he was a good driver too. That was when I realized I trusted Jack, more than I ever had in my life, so I put my life in his hands and dozed off as he drove off.

I woke up to a loud bang against the car. It took me a minute to take in my surroundings. We were on Mockingbird Road, only a few streets down from my house. I looked over at Jack to see whether he was okay and ask why he stopped. I had to do a double take when I saw how the left side of Jack's car was crushed into a tree. Jack was bleeding and had a few cuts on his face. He was unconscious.

"Jack, Jack!" I yelled.

I looked around because I'd never expected this to happen. This happened only in movies. I'd never met anyone who'd been in a car crash, and I definitely didn't know what to do if I'd ever gotten in one. I looked outside of the window to see that the street was conveniently deserted. I picked up my phone to call the ambulance until I realized Jack wasn't supposed to be driving with me. We weren't supposed to be ditching school. Could I really put these things over Jack's health? Would he hate me for calling the ambulance? I had to remember to hide any evidence of our trip to Thrillpark. I dialed 9-1-1.

ack was taken away to the hospital as I hid behind a tree nearby. I chickened out at the end. I knew that if I'd been there, then the police would've questioned me and realized that we'd ditched school to go Thrillpark. I took my backpack with any evidence of Thrillpark out of the car. I hated myself for making it seem that it had just been Jack in the car instead of both of us, but I knew if we'd been caught together, someone—whether it was my parents or the school—would convince us not to be together and give me the whole rundown of how we were just stupid teenagers in love.

I walked away from the scene as they loaded Jack onto a stretcher and into the back of an ambulance. I prayed that he'd be okay, and as much as it hurt me, it felt like that was the most I could do. Then I put in my earbuds and swung my backpack over my shoulder so that, to everyone else, I looked like an average teenager walking home from school.

The guilt burdened me, and I walked home slower and slower.

Even though I just assumed that everything was going to be okay, just like it was in most movies, life wasn't a movie. What if

Jack's injuries were serious? What if he wouldn't get to play basketball ever again? What if he'd never snowboard or drive and feel the sensation of freedom I knew he craved? The worst thought crept up on me as if I hadn't known it was there all along, but it was: what if this was just like one of those movies where the love interest died? Was that really the craziest thing?

I found my heart telling my legs to run fast, faster than they'd ever run before. I had to escape the thought that haunted me the most: what if Jack died and it was all my fault?

I'd never actually been in a hospital except for when I was born. I went to the front desk because it wasn't like I could roam the halls in hopes of finding Jack without getting lost. I regretted my decision when the woman behind the desk looked up at me. She had one of those *you better not bother me or else* looks, but I decided to take some risks, because that seemed to be the theme of the day.

"Hi, I was wondering if you knew where Jack Walker was."

"The jock who crashed into a tree? Are you his head cheer-leader girlfriend or something?" she asked angrily. I really should've given more thought to talking to her after seeing the look on her face.

"I'm Bella. I'm his—"

"Look, I don't care who you are, hon. The rule is if you're not family, you're not allowed in."

"I'm Bella Walker, his um . . . cousin. Please, I really need to see him. I need to know that he's okay," I pleaded.

"You caught me on a good day, Bella whatever-your-last-name-actually-is. I don't care enough to find out whether you're actually his 'um . . . cousin.'"

"Are you serious?" I asked, only because I thought her face had said it all earlier.

"Now, you go before you get me in trouble," she said. Then for the first time, she smiled.

I walked away quickly as I tried to conceal my excitement. It was only when I got to the elevator that I realized I never thanked her or got Jack's room number. In the end, maybe I did have to roam the halls in hopes of finding him. I walked around for about a minute until I saw a group of doctors running in the opposite direction. I found them really intimidating, so I didn't ask them whether they knew where I should go, but there was a doctor who looked younger than the rest of them, trailing behind. She reminded me of myself. She seemed to be the outsider and the overlooked one, which defined me up until a few months ago, up until Jack.

I caught up to her. "Hey, excuse me. I'm trying to find Jack Walker," I said, louder than I meant to. The other doctors almost turned around, but the young doctor and I were trotting down the hallway side by side, and I needed to get her attention.

She glanced down at me. "Jock who drove into the tree?"

"Yeah. Why does everyone call him that?"

"It's a small hospital, I guess, so not much happens around here. During our free time some of the doctors come up with nick-names for the patients—not that they're funny or well thought out or anything—it's just something to do, I guess." She really did remind me of myself, and it was weird because she was older than me, but something about her seemed younger; I just couldn't place it.

"Do you know what room he's in?"

"Yeah, room 443, but you're not going to find it without my help."

"You sure you're not busy?" I asked, nodding to the group of doctors ahead of us.

"Nope, I've got nothing but free time. Follow me," she said, as we swerved away from the pack of doctors and down a smaller hallway to our right. When we got to Jack's room, the doctor said, "Have fun with your boyfriend, but just a little advice: if you love him, tell him," she said. Just like that she was gone.

I opened the door to see Jack wrapped up head to toe in bandages. Even though he looked like a mummy, he was still sitting up and smiling. I wanted to run over to him and give him a big hug, but when he noticed me, his smile disappeared.

"What's wrong?" I asked.

"Nothing, Bella. I'm so sorry, about everything. I got tired, and you were right to ask me if I was going to be okay driving, because I clearly wasn't. I wanted to take a shortcut, but I took the wrong turn onto a one-way street, and some other car was speeding down the road. It wasn't going to stop, so the only thing I could do was go on the side of the road. I didn't want you to get hurt, so I just crashed on my side. I'm sorry, and you have every right to be mad at me."

"I—I love you," I said, taking the doctor's advice to heart. "I'm sorry I left you. I shouldn't have done that."

"I get it. Don't worry about it," Jack said.

During the crash, Jack's first thought was my safety, but when it was my turn to take care of Jack, I'd abandoned him. That wasn't fair of me. It wasn't fair of me that I had all of these doubts about or relationship, but most of all it wasn't fair to Jack.

"I'll make it up to you—I promise."

"You don't have to," Jack said, which only made me feel more guilty.

"I do, and I will."

I took out my phone to text Bea: *I want to have a surprise get-well-soon party for Jack. You in?*

"What are you doing?" Jack asked as he tried to glance at my screen.

I tucked my phone away as I answered, "Nothing." But the truth was I would do everything I could for Jack because otherwise, the guilt of abandoning him would make me lose Jack forever.

After visiting Jack, I found myself writing again but was pulled out of my story by a knock at the door. "Hey, Bells," my mom said.

"Hi. Do you need something?" I asked, even though I was reluctant to separate from the words forming on the screen.

"Dinner's almost ready. I just wanted to check in on you. Are you good?"

There was so much I could say. I could tell her how my life was falling apart and finally have someone to talk to, but that meant treating years of feeling like an outsider in my own family as if they were nothing. I wasn't ready for that. "Yeah, I'm good."

"Okay," she said as she turned back around to leave, only to turn back toward me. "You know what? I can't do this anymore, Bells."

"Can't do what anymore?" I asked, avoiding talking at all costs.

"I can't pretend that everything is okay and turn a blind eye to all of this. I wanted to let you figure this all out on your own, but you're sixteen, and you shouldn't have to be doing this all on your own. I want to help you, Bells. I want to help you, but I can't do that if you don't talk to me."

I looked at her for a moment. She was right about everything, to my surprise. Unlike TV shows, kids can't run around solving murders without their parents having a clue. She knew what was going on because she was my mom.

"Okay. Do you want to sit down? This might take a while." We both laughed at that, but we both knew that it was a step in the right direction. She sat at the foot of my bed, and I swiveled around to face her from my chair. I wanted to start from the beginning, but there was something else building up inside of me. "I don't think I'm ready for this, Mom, any of it. I wasn't ready for Jack. I wasn't ready to fall in love because he was right about me. I can't love him if I can't love myself. I didn't love myself when I met Jack. I thought I'd love myself if I had Jack. I thought I'd be this person I'd always wanted to be—the person I always thought you and Dad wanted me to be."

"Wait, what?" She looked at me blankly. I thought it was a joke, but she was serious.

"You were always encouraging me to be friends with Bea and the girls. I just thought you wanted me to be like them—pretty, cool, and popular and all of that."

"Oh, Bells, no. You thought that? I can't believe you thought that. It's all my fault. I love who you are, and I wouldn't change a thing. I just noticed that you were never happy with Jade, Makenzie, and Nicole, but you stuck with them anyway. I wanted you to be friends with girls who made you happy. I know Bea is a little tough at first, but once you get to know her, she's so sweet and kind. I just wanted you to surround yourself with girls like her. I was friends with girls like her in high school, and I was happy. I just thought you'd want that. I was trying to give you everything I could, but maybe that wasn't what you needed." For the first time, everything about my mom made sense. I understood what she meant about Bea and the girls. The girls had welcomed me with open arms. As for Bea, once we got close, she treated me like her best friend.

"Thank you," I told her, and it was the most genuinely I'd ever thanked her.

She smiled at me for a moment as if she understood what the thank you had meant. "But that's not all, is it?"

"How did you know?" I asked, wishing that it could be that simple.

"It never is, especially with girl drama. People think it's silly, and maybe it is sometimes, but what people on the outside don't understand is that these are your most important relationships. It's not crazy to get upset about. It's not crazy to have these emotions, Bella. It's all normal, so you can't be afraid to let it all out."

"I miss Leanne," I admitted. "Things were just so much easier then. I never told anyone what our fight was about. I always thought it was the biggest deal, but it wasn't worth it. I know that now because I finally got what I wanted, and it wasn't worth it. I ruined my friendship for nothing. I started the fight over stupidity and jealousy. I was so stupid, Mom."

"What do you mean?" Maybe I was giving my mom too much credit. She wasn't perfect.

"I started it all over Jack. Leanne knew I liked him, and she went out with him anyway. But what if there was more? What if it wasn't as simple as that?"

"You know, when I was your age, I had a Jack."

"Dad." I didn't even have to ask.

"No, actually, his name was Jesse. He went out with my best friend, Amanda, first and then broke up with her and went out with me. I, of course, got into a fight with Amanda over him. He was kind of a jerk, but I just wanted him because my best friend had him. Eventually, I realized he wasn't worth the fight and broke up with him, but I realized it was too late. Amanda wasn't willing to forgive me. I was kind of on my own for a while in high school and got to discover who I was, which I think I needed, but I could've done it with Amanda by my side. It's hard going through high school alone, but that was when I met your dad. Okay, maybe not the best example for what I'm trying to say. It's not that if you're alone in high school, you'll find the love of your life, because that's not what I'm saying—and, besides, you have so much time to do that. Okay, I'm clearly not good at this. What I'm trying to say is I wish I'd had Amanda by my side, and if there's a chance for you and Leanne to be friends, go for it."

"What if she hates me? I was awful to her."

"Why don't you go over there and see for yourself? You won't know if you never ask, and I'm not saying it's going to be easy, but it's worth a shot. I'd hate for you to go through life wondering 'what if.'"

The next day, I still didn't know whether I was ready to go talk with Leanne. Even though I'd been honest for the first time about missing her and we had a lot of memories together, it was so long since we had a conversation that I didn't know how she'd react if I just went up to her in the hallway to say hi.

I walked into my chemistry class too distracted by my thoughts about reconciling my friendship with Leanne to notice Mark sit down in the seat next to me. "So what have I missed this year?" He asked, taking me out of my thoughts. Somehow it was the most perfect thing to say. He pretended like nothing had happened from the day before, and everything was normal between us. But what I needed was a distraction and a friend to talk to, so I went back to pretending like nothing had happened at all between us and went along with his banter.

"You've been out since October, right?" I said.

"Yeah, my last day was September 28."

"Okay," I said, not even bothering to flip through my notes. "You've basically missed everything. You know how Keane is. He goofed off and barely taught in September because he claims it's a joke of a month, and we only really started learning in October."

"I didn't have Keane when I was here before. I had Townsend."

"Lucky, I heard he's really good."

"Yeah, he was, but this school decided that I didn't fulfill my first semester because my 'mountain hippie school' classes didn't fulfill the requirements here, which is kind of funny because the mountain hippie school said the same thing about this school. So, basically, what I'm trying to say is that it's almost the end of March, and this school looks at me as if I've missed six months of school. So they had to move my schedule around so that I could fulfill my requirements from both semesters in less than three months instead of ten, which just makes *so* much sense. Sorry that took so long to explain. It's just that I'm so angry about the whole thing. It's like—"

Then the bell rang, and Mr. Keane walked in. I distracted myself with drawing stick figures with sunglasses only to realize Mark had started drawing stick figures with sunglasses of his own. Except they weren't stick figures; they were like good, realistic cartoons. Why did everyone have a talent except for me?

We had our next class together, so we talked to each other on the way there. Our conversation reminded me of the way my conversations with Leanne used to be—simple and easy. Somehow Mark was able to understand exactly what I meant when I didn't know how to express myself—just like Leanne had done. I know I was comparing Grace and Leanne earlier, and it made sense, looking back, because they both betrayed me, whether they intended to or not. On the other hand, Mark hadn't betrayed me, and I couldn't see that happening anytime in the near future. I wondered why I didn't have more Marks in my life.

When we got to lunch, the first thing I noticed was that Jack wasn't waiting for me with food like he always was. He was still bandaged and sitting with Luke and the other guys as usual. Luke looked over at Mark and me and said something to the table, but Jack didn't turn around.

Mark put his hand on my shoulder. "Wanna sit with me?" he asked in a way that made it just about impossible to say no.

"Yeah, why not?" I told Mark, not expecting an answer, even though I knew there were so many reasons he could give. I looked over at Jack's table one more time and saw Luke wink at me. I guessed some things never change. I looked over at the girls' table to see Bea staring at Grace, who was talking loudly and appearing as though she was at the center of attention. She was talking up a storm, and all of the girls were listening intently.

"What, you have somewhere better to go?" Mark asked.

"Do I have anywhere better to go?" I asked, restating Mark's question. "No, no, I really don't," I said.

He started to walk toward the only empty table, which was at the edge of the cafeteria, where we would be partly shielded from the girls' table and Jack's friends' table. Mark walked with confidence that I wished I could have in the situation we'd put ourselves in, but I was more of his shadow than a human being who was walking behind him. We sat down across from each other until we realized that we hadn't gotten food. We seemed to acknowledge it at the same time, so we both stood up. From there we got our own food, which was a foreign concept to me, as I hadn't done that since February.

"You're seriously telling me that you like Bella?"

Everyone turned to see Heather, of all people, shouting at Bea. It was clear that a fight had been going on for a while now, but it wasn't anywhere near done. It was at that stage where it attracted everyone's attention because one person shouts loudly out of anger. I was used to the girls having a lot of drama, but this involved me, and for the first time, they weren't on my side. I guess I'd always thought that when the girls turned on Bea, I would be on their side. I didn't expect them to turn on her when she was on my side and fighting for me.

"Yeah, and what's so wrong with that?" Bea fought back.

"You want to know what's wrong with that?" It was Mila this time. "Bella just uses people. She used Leanne to get to Jack, and she used Jack to get to us."

"Bella," Mark whispered. "Let's get outta here."

Mark was trying to rescue me. As much as I wanted to be whisked off, why did I need to be rescued? I only needed to be rescued if everything Mila just said was true, and it wasn't. But was that what everyone really thought? What if everyone was right about me being opportunistic? "No," I told Mark, convincing myself that it was the right thing to say.

"What do you mean, 'no'?"

"Running off would show them that what they're saying about me is true, but it's not." I surprised both of us with my courage.

I turned my attention back to the fight that was occupying everyone else's attention. Heather was yelling at Bea again. "I don't understand how all of a sudden Leanne isn't this bad person you've made her out to be all year. You're the one who called her the sophomore slut, but then, all of a sudden, she's this victim and deserves to be with her true love? You can't just twist the truth only when it benefits you!"

"Yeah, that was a messed up thing to do, and I'm trying to fix that," Bea shouted back. I could tell Bea wasn't winning this fight, and I silently rooted for her. "I can't do this anymore," Bea said, getting up. "Bella is our friend, and you can't just turn on her like that . . . I can't be friends with the type of people who do that."

"Then don't be," Grace dared her. That's when the truth occurred to me. I had no doubt that Grace had somehow orchestrated the fight so that they would all turn on Bea. I turned to look at the boys' table, and they were all staring at the girls. Jack wasn't smiling, but his face was fixed on Grace, and his blue eyes were cold. Whether or not Jack really did lose his memory, I wondered whether he and Grace were perfect for each other after all.

Mark wrapped his arm around me, not aware of the countless rumors it would start, and started to guide me out of the lunchroom. I stopped him. Bea was getting up from the table as the other girls were yelling and glaring at her. I remembered our last fight and how Bea mentioned how hard it was for people to truly change. Bea was braver than I was. She always cared about other people — even if that meant sometimes she cared too much about what they thought — and right now she was willing to throw that all away.

Bea left the cafeteria, and I wanted to follow her. I wasn't like Bea — I thought about only how other people would benefit or hurt me. Maybe that was a side effect of how I didn't know myself or love myself. I shimmied my way out of Mark's touch. When I caught a look at his face, he was smiling. Was I so desperate to not be by myself that I would keep hanging out with Mark, despite everything? "You better get back to Grace and whatever game you're still playing," I said. I left to follow Bea. I needed to start figuring out the ways I could be a better friend, and maybe that way I could truly start thinking better of myself too.

After school that day, I found myself on Leanne's doorstep. She was the one person whom I'd felt free with—that is, until we'd stopped talking. As I rang Leanne's doorbell, though, I thought that I'd try to make loving Leanne just one more reason to love myself, instead of feeling trapped.

As soon as she opened the door, I wished I hadn't pushed the doorbell. She was standing there with her heavy makeup and blond highlights that seemed unfamiliar, yet behind all of it I could still see her warm brown eyes. "Hey, Leanne," I said. I wished I hadn't come to her doorstep, and I wished I could turn back time—but wishing for those impossible things was just another way to disappear, like a kid into a fantasy.

Then a strange thing happened. As Leanne drew me into a hug—one of those warm Leanne hugs I didn't realize I'd missed so much—time did seem to turn backward. All our memories came rushing back—our years of friendship, inside jokes, nicknames, fights, make-ups, and talks. It was like no time had passed between us at all.

"Come inside," she said, pushing open the front door. I followed her to the couch that I'd sat on thousands of times, whether it was for a movie night or just one of our deep talks that I missed so much. Leanne plopped herself in her usual corner, and I did the same in my corner. I appreciated the fact that she remembered, and I knew she probably felt the same.

Her dog, Ned, a huge German Shepard mix, scampered across the living room to Leanne's side. Leanne loved that dog to death, while I, on the other hand, had evolved from scared to death to almost tolerant of Ned. After Ned got his usual pat on the head, he walked over to me, sniffed my leg, and walked back to Leanne as if he remembered that I only almost tolerated him, which I appreciated. But Ned moved slower than I remembered, and he flopped onto the ground by Leanne's feet. Ned had gotten old. "So what brings you here?" Leanne said, trying to sound casual.

"I wanted to say I'm sorry," I said.

"For what?"

"For everything. For how we stopped being friends. For going along with the rumors everyone else said about you."

Leanne stared at Ned, then back at me. "I'm sorry too, Bells. But let's forget about it." She smiled.

Hearing her call me by my nickname made me smile too, and it brought me back to our old times again. We sunk deeper into the sofa cushions. Then a weird thought came to me. "I think I just went through exactly what you went through," I said.

Leanne laughed. "You mean with Jack and Mark? Yeah, it was interesting watching a rerun of my life from the sidelines, I have to say." She looked over at me. "Not that your life is a rerun, I meant—"

I put my hand over my face and laughed too. "No, it was exactly like a rerun, wasn't it? With Jack and Mark and Grace— even the actors were exactly the same."

Leanne rolled her eyes. "Forget them."

I thought about what my mom had said, about not having to go through high school alone. In the past few months, I'd been trying to figure out Jack's story, and Mark's story, and Grace's story, all the while finding my own story. But I'd never asked Leanne for hers. "I want to hear how you've been doing," I said.

She looked over at me. "Bad," she said. We burst out laughing again.

"I want to hear your story," I said. "I want to hear everything."

About the Author

*E*velyn Landy lives in New York City. She will graduate from high school in 2020 and plans to pursue screenwriting in college. She has attended writing programs at Brandeis University and New York University. Her short fiction has been distinguished by the Alliance of Young Artists & Writers. Aside from her interests in written and cinematic storytelling, she enjoys spending time with her family and playing with her dog, Buddy.

www.evelynlandy.com